MW00513946

LAST TO TELL

PAUL J. TEAGUE

ALSO BY PAUL J. TEAGUE

Morecambe Bay Trilogy 1

Book 1 - Left For Dead

Book 2 - Circle of Lies

Book 3 - Truth Be Told

Morecambe Bay Trilogy 2

Book 4 - Trust Me Once

Book 5 - Fall From Grace

Book 6 - Bound By Blood

Morecambe Bay Trilogy 3

Book 7 - First To Die

Book 8 - Nothing To Lose

Book 9 - Last To Tell

Note: The Morecambe Bay trilogies are best read in the order shown above.

Don't Tell Meg Trilogy

Features DCI Kate Summers and Steven Terry.

Book 1 - Don't Tell Meg

Book 2 - The Murder Place

Book 3 - The Forgotten Children

Standalone Thrillers

Dead of Night

One Last Chance

ONE

'I can save her, but I need your permission to do this—'

'To do what?' Will asked, his face white with shock. 'Last time I saw you, you were about to torture us. It's only because of Charlotte that I didn't kill you that day. Now you want me to trust you?'

Henderson didn't look at Will as he spoke. Instead, he ignored the panic around him and pushed down on Charlotte's chest, giving her the compressions which might spark her heart back into life.

'If you wait and let the ambulance crew attend to her, she may well die. If we do this my way, I can help her—'

'Dad, come on, we have to move quickly—' Olli urged.

Milo comforted Lucia but was primed to do whatever was needed on the doctor's word.

'Can you drive?' Henderson asked. He looked up long enough to let Milo know he was addressing him.

'Sure—'

Henderson threw him his fob, which he pulled out of his pocket.

'Take the Tesla in the car park by The Station pub. Bring it around the back of the fair. Stay away from the cops. Okay?'

Milo nodded, took Lucia's hand, and they ran off.

'What can we do?' Olli asked.

Henderson continued his chest compressions.

'There's a defibrillator at the back of the Festival Market; get it for me. You'll have to call emergency services for a code. Give them false information—'

'But—' Olli began.

'Do it,' Henderson instructed.

'What about me?' Will asked. 'You promise me you can save her?'

'I can't promise you,' Henderson replied, 'but I can tell you that by the time an ambulance gets here, your wife has no chance of making it out alive. I worked as a medic in Iraq in 1991. I'm going to treat your wife like a casualty of war. That's the only way she'll survive this.'

Henderson's voice was calm and in control. Will latched onto it in his panic, like a guide rope leading him through a treacherous path.

'Once I finish these compressions, I want you to help me move your wife out of sight. We have to be fast. Then you're going to put the police off the scent—'

'What? I can't do that—'

'You want your wife to live?'

'Yes, of course—'

'Then, do as I say. Your wife's DCI friend will help to smooth things over. We have to keep your wife out of the hospital.'

Henderson finished his compressions then signalled to Will to take Charlotte's legs. He grabbed her arms. He counted aloud to mark the time. If he was going to save her, they were all on the clock.

'Okay, enough,' he said once they'd moved her out of sight, behind a hamburger stall.

'Now get over to where that electrician is out cold and make sure he gets medical attention. I'd guess he has a concussion; he'll be fine, I think. Tell the police the man who did this got away and don't mention your wife—'

'That's perverting the course of justice—'

'For Christ's sake,' Henderson snapped for the first time. 'Just do it!'

Chastened, Will kneeled to kiss Charlotte.

'You make sure she lives, or I swear, I'll lead the police directly to your door,' he said, placing himself in front of Henderson.

'She'll pull through,' Henderson assured him, 'Now go, make sure the cops stay away from this area long enough for me to get your wife into my Tesla.'

Will looked at Henderson and then at Charlotte. He took a deep breath, then did as he was told.

Henderson looked up to see that Milo had already driven his Tesla around the back of the fairground. Milo had spotted him already and gave a wave from behind the steering wheel. Olli was in the car too and didn't wait for the car to stop before leaping out of the back door and running towards the wire fencing.

'Where do you want the defibrillator?' he shouted.

'I need my bag out the back too,' Henderson replied. 'Throw it over. Careful, just drop it over the fence.'

Olli did as he was told, then returned moments later with a bag. By this time, Milo had prised a gap between the fence panels and squeezed his way through with Lucia and Willow behind him.

'I told Olli to hop into the back of the car; it was quicker,' he said. 'How's it going?'

'I need your help. What's your name?'

'Milo—'

'Carry on with the chest compressions; I'll talk you through it. Don't be gentle, push as hard as you can—'

'What about the mouth to mouth thing?'

'Not necessary, just do the compressions.'

Henderson rummaged in his bag and brought out a syringe pack which he hastily assembled.

'What are you going to do?' Lucia asked, sobbing. She was calm now, watching the doctor working on her mother, in a state of suspended panic.

'I'm going to administer adrenaline,' Henderson replied. 'This is not quite how they'd do it at the infirmary, but this will sort your mother out. It's a little unconventional, but it works wonders.'

Henderson continued setting up the materials in his bag, all the time encouraging Milo with the compressions.

'Go and see what's going on with the cops,' he said to Olli and Willow. 'Don't give it away that we're over here.'

Olli said nothing. He and Willow went through the gap in the fence and ran around the perimeter toward the fairground entrance to conceal where they'd come from.

Henderson assembled the defibrillator kit and instructed Milo to stand back.

'I want you two to get the car ready to transport Charlotte, okay?'

'But I want to help,' Milo protested.

'You are helping,' Henderson continued. He moved in close to whisper. 'I don't want her kids to see what happens next. That's her daughter, I take it?'

Milo nodded.

'What happens next?' Milo whispered back.

'Let's put it this way, this kind of thing is best left in war zones. It's effective, but disturbing to watch. Get yourselves out of here, I need to work fast.'

Milo did as he was told. Henderson heard him distracting Lucia. He was a good kid, he caught on quickly.

Since becoming involved with Morecambe's criminal fraternity, very little fazed Henderson. He thought he'd seen it all in Iraq: severed limbs, shrapnel wounds and soldiers who were supposed to be dead. Criminals came with their distinctive injuries: torture wounds, damaged internal organs, and drugs overdoses. He was paid so much money because his record was exemplary, his methods unconventional, and his service discreet.

Henderson was not in the habit of losing people. If they could be saved, he would save them. As he set about bringing the life back to Charlotte, he checked his watch; it had to be now, or she wasn't going to make it. The risk of brain damage was too high; the medics would have lost her. It was a damn good job he'd followed her into the fairground.

Five minutes later, Olli and Willow returned, this time approaching from inside the fairground. Henderson was hunched over Charlotte; he'd turned her on her side, her entire body was motionless. Discarded at his side was an empty syringe; the defibrillator had been thrown clear of her body.

'Oh my God, she's not dead, is she?' Olli asked, stopping in his tracks. 'Tell me she's okay, please.'

Charlotte's right foot twitched slightly as Milo and Lucia re-joined them through the gap in the fence.

Charlotte was almost motionless on the ground. But her eyes were slightly open and her fingers moving, as if she'd just begun to inhabit a new body and was getting used to its feel.

'She's alive, she made it through okay,' Henderson began. 'Now, let's get her out of here to a place where she can recover. She's been on one hell of a ride.'

TWO

Charlotte listened to the voices for several minutes before she recognised who they belonged to. She was unable to open her eyes, her body was gripped by fatigue. She was disorientated as if it were an out-of-body experience. She could hear what was being said but was unable to take part in the conversation. She wondered for a moment if she was dead.

'DCI Summers is downstairs.'

It was Olli. He was talking to somebody whose voice she couldn't place.

'Best get this over with,' came the reply.

'Kate will be okay. She'll just be grateful you saved her.'

That was Will's voice. The last thing she remembered was Will sounding distraught as if something terrible had happened. She jumped; was Lucia okay?

'Steady, Charlotte,' came the unfamiliar voice. It was Doctor Henderson. She'd just been talking to him, hadn't she?

Charlotte tried to move her fingers. She wasn't dead

because they responded. She could feel them brushing against a crisp sheet.

She moved on to her eyelids; they were so heavy. She willed them to open like it was some challenging exercise she was trying to complete at the gym.

'She's awake, everybody,' came Henderson's voice. 'Just give her a moment, she's going to be confused. Lucia, pass me that bottle of water, will you.'

At the mention of water, Charlotte realised that her mouth felt like it was filled with dry sand. She tried to speak, but her voice would not come. A confident hand trickled drops of water onto her lips, then into her mouth. Her mouth moistened, like a desert in the rain. She moved her jaw and attempted to say something. It just came out as a croak.

Her eyes were beginning to focus now. She was in her bedroom at the guest house, that much she could tell. It was bright - daytime - and there were people there, sitting around on chairs, talking among themselves.

'Gently does it,' came the doctor's voice again. 'Just take your time, you've just had one hell of a shock. Don't rush yourself.'

Charlotte turned slowly so that she could see the other side of her bed. There was medical equipment there; she might have been in a hospital room for all she knew.

'What's going on?'

Her voice was hesitant and weak, but she succeeded in making herself understood.

'You were on the receiving end of an electric shock. Fortunately, the voltage wasn't so high. But, it was enough to stop your heart for a while. We managed to get you jump-started again, so everything is fine now—'

Charlotte heard Will's voice, but she couldn't see him in the room.

'That's understating it a bit,' he said. 'Doctor Henderson here has been bringing me up-to-date with your escapades. You didn't mention being burned alive in a coffin last time we spoke.'

Charlotte made a poor attempt at a smile. Her lips were still dry. They felt like they would crack if she forced them too much. Will was teasing her; he was not scolding her. That would come later, no doubt. He just sounded relieved, as if he was on a high. If what the doctor said was true, then she figured she'd just escaped with her life.

The last thing she remembered was the man holding the cable. She couldn't figure out why he was holding it like that. He'd dropped it, then she'd heard voices in a state of panic. And now, here she was.

'What happened to the guy?'

She forced out another sentence.

'You're on bed rest,' Will said. 'Forget the guy, he's no longer your problem.'

Charlotte moved her mouth to give a reply, then thought better of it. The bedroom door opened, and she heard Kate's voice. Charlotte was struggling to hang onto the threads of conversation; she kept drifting in and out.

'May I speak to Charlotte in private?' she heard Kate ask.

'You must go easy,' the doctor replied. 'She's not out of the woods yet.'

Charlotte was aware of the room being vacated around her. She heard Olli again, then Lucia. It must have been serious if the entire family was gathered around her bed. Will was the last to go.

'I know you're a police officer,' he began, 'but I don't want Charlotte involved anymore. That's her lot. It's over for her.'

Charlotte waited for him to leave the room. Her mouth had dried up again, and she forced more words out of her mouth.

'That's what he thinks,' she managed to say.

Kate kissed Charlotte on her forehead and took her hand. Charlotte sensed her taking a seat at the side of the bed.

'He's right, you know,' Kate replied. 'This is too much, Charlotte. We almost lost you. This can't happen again. You've been out cold for hours.'

Even lying there in the bed, almost motionless because she couldn't yet figure out how to make her body move, Charlotte knew it wasn't over. Not until that bastard was caught or dead. Then it would be over.

'I can hear your mind whirring,' Kate said. 'Don't even think about it. The police are dealing with this now. It's entirely in their hands.'

'Sure,' was all Charlotte could manage to say.

'Doctor Henderson told me not to take too long,' Kate continued, 'But I wanted to deliver the good news personally.'

'You got him?'

The coordination was returning to Charlotte's mouth. She wished she could roll over to take a swig of water.

'No, he got away. It's almost better news than that.'

Kate picked up the bottle of water at the side of the bed.

'Do you want some of this?' she asked.

Charlotte gave a small nod.

Kate held it to her lips, and Charlotte took a decent drink. It felt immediately better.

'So, what do you know already?' Kate asked.

'Nothing,' Charlotte replied. Her voice was coming back now.

'Okay. So, the bad guy got away. Again. The motorcycle he's using isn't registered anywhere. Well, it was, but he appears to have taken it from a scrapyard. So, we can't trace him. And your chap in Saltburn. He can't give us the guy's name. He does casual work at the arcade, cash-in-hand. He admitted he was phoning his mate to warn him that you were snooping around. He only knows him as Jim—'

'What about the JI on the phone?'

'Jim - that's all we got. No surname. He knows him as JI or Jim. He lives in a squat in Saltburn. We've nothing more than that.'

'Is nothing simple?' Charlotte groaned.

'That's not what I'm here to tell you,' Kate continued, renewed enthusiasm in her voice.

'Guess who's back on the case?'

'What? How?'

'Well, it's good news and bad news. DCI Comfort managed to secure the address of Josh Irving through official channels. He's got a new identity, and the powers that be have given their permission for us to contact him in connection with this case.'

'So how does that put you back in charge?'

Charlotte could feel the life creeping back into her body as Kate updated her on the latest developments.

'DCI Comfort made a big cock-up. He thought he was sending over the details to the Police Commissioner on Facebook Messenger. That's a big no-no, it's strictly forbidden. But, instead of communicating Josh's new identity in a private message, he posted it on his Facebook page. He's in deep shit, and the Police and Crime Commissioner backed down over me being reinstated. I'm back in action. Now, I'm going to nail the piece of shit who did this to you.'

THREE

Frank Allan's radio crackled into life.

'Control to CH11'

'CH11 uncommitted, go ahead,' he replied, raising his eyebrows at his colleague. Larry Schofield took a final gulp of his tea and sat expectantly, awaiting details of the incoming job.

'CH11 reports of a disturbance at The Travellers Rest public house. Can you attend?'

'CH11 en route,' Frank responded, grimacing at PC Schofield.

'It's been non-stop today, Larry. It's like there's something in the air. The locals can't keep their hands in their pockets.'

'Well, it keeps us both in a job,' Larry replied.

Frank picked up the two cups and looked inside Larry's.

'You were supposed to be cutting back on the sugar. There are at least two teaspoons in there. I thought we had a deal on eating healthier.'

Larry picked up his helmet and positioned it on his head.

'I know, I know. Middle age is creeping up on us. But I don't have a family like you, I don't have the same incentive. And it's hard, you know. I used to take three sugars in my tea. Two is quite a reduction.'

Frank handed over the cups at the cafe counter and thanked the owner. They'd only managed to grasp a short break, but at least it had broken the shift. It was always a busy Saturday when Morecambe F.C. lost a game. The combination of alcohol and The Shrimps' elevation to the Conference League had upped the stakes for the locals. It meant that a Saturday shift pounding the streets was non-stop once the game had finished.

'I was hoping to get back to spend some time with my kids,' Frank said, as they exited the Arndale and took a turn in the direction of The Travellers Rest. 'They're growing up so fast, and I'm always torn between taking overtime to pay the bills and spending more time at home. Kate needs her mother, she's at that age—'

'Come on, Frank, you're doing the best you can,' Larry answered, with a look on his face that suggested they'd had this conversation before. 'The kids will scrape by, you're managing okay. After your Evie died, I don't know how you all held it together. Cut yourself some slack; you're doing fine.'

It was a short distance to the pub, but long enough for Frank to reflect on his imminent move to Detective Constable. It would take him away from the endless round of domestic incidents, pub brawls and break-ins. He hoped it might place him out of harm's way; as sole carer for Brett and Kate, he couldn't afford to get injured. The kids were his priority; policing could be a hazardous occupation.

They reached the pub. There was a small group standing outside. Experience told Frank this was usually a sign of the less inebriated drinkers moving out of the way to avoid trouble going on inside.

'CH11 to Control,' Frank spoke into his radio.

'Go ahead, CH11.'

'CH11, we've arrived at The Travellers Rest. Just about to enter.'

'CH11 obliged.'

'Okay, Larry, let's see what joys await us.'

Frank took a deep breath. There was a time when he had relished the adrenalin of such encounters, but since finding himself a single parent, he'd never been so aware of how vulnerable it made him. He liked working with Larry and didn't particularly care to split up the partnership. But, Larry was a beat bobby through and through, and after a couple of failed attempts at his Sergeant's exam, he had resigned himself to a career on the streets.

'I've only got to survive until I'm fifty-five,' he'd joke to Frank. 'Then I'll take my pension and retire somewhere quiet; hopefully without any injuries. I'll get myself a boat and a dog, which will suit me fine.'

If only it were so simple for Frank.

He pushed through the solid door which led to the public bar; the aggravation seldom broke out on the lounge side. He sensed the tension the moment the door swung open.

'Get ya fuckin' hands off me—'

Frank recognised the voice.

'It's Jonny Irving again,' he sighed at Larry. He spoke into his radio again.

'CH11 Control.'

'Go ahead, CH11.'

'CH11, we've got this one.'

'CH11 thanking you.'

'Okay, Jonny, that's enough,' Larry said, walking over to Irving. He was holding a pint of lager in one hand and a pool cue in the other. A group of three men were surrounding him, their fists clenched and poised for aggression. They relaxed as the two officers put some space between the two hostile parties.

'I'll take the pool cue,' Frank said, grasping it with one hand and waiting for Jonny to release it to him.

'So, what's this all about?' Frank asked.

'That bastard spilt ma girl's drink—' he began.

'It was an accident,' one of the other men interrupted. 'This crazy bugger jumps up and starts threatening us with a pool cue.'

Sitting behind Jonny was a woman who seemed cut from the same cloth as him. She had a hard look in her eyes like she was a survivor. She had a full glass in front of her.

'My mate bought her a new drink. Look, she's barely touched it.'

'Okay, guys, I see what's going on here. Make yourselves scarce for five minutes, will you? We'll take Jonny home, I think he's had enough for the day.'

Jonny had now released the pool cue and placed his glass on the table, in front of the woman. Frank placed the cue onto the nearby pool table.

'Yer come fer a quiet drink and all yer get is trouble,' Jonny muttered.

'We're taking you home, Jonny, you've had enough for today,' Larry said. 'Now, are you going to come quietly, or are you going to make this difficult for us?'

Frank walked over from the pool table and back to Larry's side. The three men dispersed. They weren't happy about it, but it was only their male pride that was hurt; Frank figured they'd survive.

Frank remained alert as he watched Jonny's face. He could see the drunkard was figuring out whether to escalate things or back down.

'Leave it, Jonny,' the woman said. 'It's not worth it.'

Jonny relaxed, and Larry and Frank followed suit.

'We'll walk him home and make sure he doesn't get into any more trouble,' Frank said to the woman. 'Are you the landlady?' he called over to the bar.

'That's me, for my sins,' a middle-aged woman replied. She looked like she'd seen it all before.

'Any damage caused here?' Frank asked.

'No, but I'd be grateful if he didn't come in here again. He gets pissed like that every time. He's a pain in my arse.'

'Noted,' Larry chipped in.

Frank guided Jonny toward the door.

'Carry on enjoying your afternoon,' he said to the remaining customers. 'I'm sorry that you were disturbed—'

'Aye, fuck off the lot o' yer!' Jonny called out.

Frank and Larry took an arm each and marched him out of the pub.

'It's safe to go back in now,' Larry announced to the group who'd been waiting outside.

Frank updated Control as to their movements.

'We're walking you back home, Jonny,' he explained once he'd signed off. 'I suggest you sleep it off today, you've had quite enough booze for one day. Are you still living on the estate?'

Jonny Irving was well-known to the local bobbies. He was one of many habitual trouble-makers in the resort. He never did anything sufficiently bad to go to prison, but he got into enough scrapes to be a nuisance. The worst-case scenario for Jonny Irving was a night sleeping it off in police cells. But Frank wanted to avoid that; he knew through the grapevine that Jonny had children at home.

It was a slow walk back to Jonny's house. The further they walked, the more incoherent Jonny became. By the time they reached his house on the estate, they'd had to take an arm each to support him.

'Gently does it when we knock at the door,' Frank warned. 'I don't want to worry the kids more than we need to.'

Frank tapped at the door while Larry supported Jonny. There was movement inside. After some time, the door opened. It was the eldest boy, Frank didn't know his name. What he had heard was that social services was sniffing around the family. He didn't want to make things worse for them. He'd seen for himself how fast family life could fray at the seams.

'Hello, son, I'm afraid your dad has had a bit too much to drink—'

'Get upstairs,' the boy called into the house. Frank saw a younger boy and a girl making their way to the staircase.

'Where can we put him?' Larry asked.

'Just lay him on the sofa,' the boy replied. 'He can piss himself all he wants to there.'

Frank surveyed the hallway and lounge as they steered Jonny toward the sofa. No wonder social services was on their case. The house smelled of urine. The kids looked like their clothes hadn't been ironed. The carpet was disgusting and didn't appear to have seen a vacuum cleaner in years. Frank might have felt like he was failing as a father, but at least his kids didn't live like this.

Larry and Frank lay Jonny down on the sofa, and he began to snore.

'Will you be alright, son?' Frank asked. 'He'll stay asleep now until he sobers up.'

The boy nodded. He looked like he was fighting back tears.

'If you need any help, just call the police station. Okay?'

Frank looked around. He couldn't see a telephone anywhere. There was a rent arrears notice from the council on a food-stained coffee table.

The boy wanted them out of the house. Frank took a final look around, then ushered Larry toward the door. The boy shut it behind them like he was pleased to see them gone.

'Poor kids,' Larry began, 'Imagine having a father like that.'

'I thought Jonny Irving's wife had left him,' Frank replied, thinking back to the scene at the pub. 'So, who the hell was that woman he was drinking with?'

FOUR

Charlotte tried to sit up in bed. Her body felt like it hadn't moved for a week.

'Oh, Jesus, what happened to me at that fairground? I feel terrible.'

'As far as I can tell, Charlotte, you're a very lucky woman,' Kate told her. 'I got so excited about my news, I've barely stopped to ask how you are. I can see you're still alive; that's a good start, I suppose.'

'My body feels like it's given up on me. My mind feels okay; that electric shock doesn't appear to have erased any files. You are my daughter, Lucia, aren't you?'

Kate stared at Charlotte a moment, then laughed.

'You had me worried for a moment there. At least your sense of humour hasn't gone—'

'You know I don't want to step down from this case, don't you?' Charlotte interrupted, as serious now as she'd ever been. 'This is personal. He can't do that to me and expect me to turn the other cheek.'

'Charlotte, you can't. Look at the state of you. I'll be

pushing you around in a wheelchair at this rate. Have you spoken to Will yet?'

Charlotte thought it over for a few seconds. She didn't recall having it out with Will yet. She wanted to talk to Henderson, too. If anyone could get her back up on her feet, it was him.

'I don't think I've had that pleasure yet,' she replied.

'Well, when he came down to meet me in the downstairs hallway just now, he was furious with me. I didn't know he could get as angry as that. He was blaming me for getting you caught up in a load of trouble again. I don't want to be the one responsible for your marriage imploding.'

'He's just frustrated,' Charlotte explained. 'He gets angry when he feels like he can't do anything to help. He's just concerned about me, that's all. But I'm not stopping, Kate; I have to see this through to the end now.'

Kate looked at her and squeezed her hand.

'I thought you'd say that,' she frowned. 'I feel the same way. We're getting close to finding out what happened to my dad. I can't stop. And now I'm back on the case, well, we have full access to the latest information.'

Charlotte thought about DCI Comfort. He'd always seemed like a good guy to her. What a way to land himself in hot water; she'd made similar errors with social media in the past, but never with stakes so high.

'What will happen to DCI Comfort?' Charlotte asked. 'Will he lose his job?'

'I doubt that,' Kate answered, 'but he'll have to spend some time in the wilderness, just like I did after the Fabian Armstrong affair. He's a good copper; I hope he won't have to fall on his sword.'

'What do we know about the kids' identities then?'

Charlotte began. 'Or, should I just read about it on Facebook?'

Kate made a pained expression.

'Ouch, that's a nasty burn,' she scolded. 'We know Josh Irving's new name. It's better than we could have hoped. You'll never believe it too; he's a writer. Talk about living in plain sight. He has a holiday home somewhere in the area; we're just getting that information confirmed. But, he's alive and well and has even made a bit of a name for himself. Who would have thought?'

'Do you think he's in touch with Seth and the others?' Charlotte suggested.

'Who knows? We'll find out once we've secured permission to speak with him—'

'You know I want in on that?' Charlotte interrupted. 'For the newspaper. He'll keep his anonymity. But what a scoop. It would be amazing.'

'Steady,' Kate warned, 'let's not run before we can walk—'

The bedroom door opened, and Doctor Henderson walked in, with Will following close behind.

'I'm going to advise that Charlotte gets some rest now,' Henderson instructed. 'She's a fortunate woman, I don't want us to push our luck any more than we have already.'

Kate took the hint and stood up.

'I'll be in touch,' she whispered. 'Oh, and I need to tell you about Dad's notebook, too. I picked it up from the parcel depot. I've had a quick flick through it—'

'Okay, that's enough now,' Henderson intervened. 'Will, might I have a moment alone with your wife? I just need to carry out some medical checks?'

Will nodded. Charlotte could see that he was reluctant. She watched as Kate and her husband left the room.

'So, what's the diagnosis, doc?' Charlotte asked. 'Will I live?'

Henderson pulled up a chair at the side of the bed and started to work through his medical checks.

'You're a very lucky lady, Charlotte, I hope you appreciate that. I haven't told your family how I brought you back, but let's just say it involved some veterinary drugs which aren't supposed to be used in human medicine—'

'I wondered why I kept wanting to go outside for a gallop,' Charlotte grinned.

'It's serious, Charlotte. Nobody can know what I did to bring you back. It's highly illegal, but it does the job. It's safe too, I hasten to add. I'd go to prison if anybody found out what I was up to.'

'I think that ship has sailed already, don't you?' Charlotte replied. She rolled over on one side to reach out for the glass of water. Her chest felt like it was on fire.

'Ow, damn, that's uncomfortable,' she winced.

'Here,' Henderson said, lifting the glass of water to her mouth.

'Look, Doctor, let's speak frankly, shall we?' she began, after taking a long sip. 'As far as I'm concerned, you and I are more than quits after our earlier altercation with Vinnie Mace. I can forgive the threat of torture in exchange for bringing me back from the dead. I'd say that's a fair deal. I trust you, okay?'

Henderson nodded.

'You do what you have to do, and I'll accept that you know what you're doing. I saw your medical certificates while I was sneaking around your house, remember? So what if your bedside manner is a little unconventional; I'm still alive, and that's good enough for me, right?'

'Thank you,' Henderson replied. 'You know, I've saved

a lot of lives like this. Off the books, no records kept, and usually bad guys. I can't tell you how good it feels to be saving one of the good guys again. It's been a while.'

Charlotte looked at him, picking the right timing to make her request.

'I'm pleased you feel that way,' she began, 'because I want you to work more of your medical magic. I've got things to do, and I can't be stuck in this bed recovering for weeks. I need you to whip me up a cocktail of meds that will get me back on my feet again. I have to get out of here. The sooner, the better.'

FIVE

Whatever Doctor Henderson was giving her, it worked. Charlotte was not ready to be up and about, but she'd shaken the overwhelming fatigue that she had felt after her encounter. Henderson warned her about overexertion and the possible side effects of the drugs he was giving her.

'If it was your mum or your wife who needed this treatment, would you do the same thing?' she asked him, at the point where she became overwhelmed by the information he was giving her.

'Yes, without hesitation,' he replied.

'Then it's fine by me,' she confirmed. 'As far as I'm concerned, I died already. What you've given me is a bonus. I am not prepared to let that man get away with it. Kate and I have his scent, and I want to do anything I can to bring him to justice. So, if it's good enough for your loved ones, it's fine by me.'

Henderson gave her a cardboard box stuffed with plastic strips packed with drugs. She was unable to read any of the words on the box. It looked Chinese or Korean to her. The doctor advised her on which drugs to take and when.

'I want you to stay plugged into that machine until I come and check you tomorrow, okay?'

Charlotte nodded.

'Agreed. And thank you, by the way. I mean it. I didn't see that electric shock coming. I still can't believe how fast it was. I'm just grateful to be here. Consider your debt to me and my husband now paid in full—'

'I'm not sure your husband feels the same way—'

'He will when I explain it to him.'

Doctor Henderson repeated his instructions for her ongoing treatment, and Will came back into the room as Henderson left. The two men exchanged a few words, and Henderson was on his way. Will took the seat closest to the bed.

'I thought we'd lost you,' he said gently. 'I feel furious with you at the moment, but I'm also so glad that you're still alive. I can't believe what that man did. I still think you should be in hospital, though.'

Charlotte talked Will through everything that had happened. She could see from his flared nostrils that he was struggling to contain his anger, but she figured it was fair enough. They had promised not to keep secrets from each other, and she'd failed miserably once again.

'Look, Will, you know I don't go looking for this trouble, right? It comes to me—'

'But you don't do much to steer clear of it either—'

'We're not the bad guys, Will. Remove the bad guys, and the problem goes away. Imagine what it's like for Kate. She deals with these scumbags every day of her life.'

'Yes, but she doesn't seem to get into the same scrapes as you do.'

'If it wasn't for Kate and Doctor Henderson, I would not be speaking to you now. Just remember that.'

Will was silent and looked out of the bedroom window as he pondered.

'Is it over now? I mean, you are going to rest, aren't you?'

It was Charlotte's turn to look out of the window now.

'I can't promise you that, Will. Kate is desperate to find out what happened to her dad. We're so close to finding this man and—'

She was about to mention that they now knew Josh's new identity. She considered sharing the information but decided instead that it was confidential to the case. After DCI Comfort's cack-handed use of Facebook, Josh was already in some danger.

'At least promise me you'll let the police deal with apprehending this guy. You can't go chasing after him, not after what happened. What if your heart gives out—'

Will's eyes teared up. He rubbed them with his hand.

'I love you, Charlotte. When I thought we'd lost you ... I just can't imagine my life without you in it.'

'I know,' she said gently. 'I'm sorry it gave you all a scare. I didn't intend to tackle him on my own. I called the police and was waiting for them to get there. He caught me by surprise.'

'We followed you in,' Will explained. 'We were walking along the promenade, and I saw the doctor tailing you into the fairground. I thought he was chasing you at first. When I saw you lying in that puddle—'

'It's over, Will. I'm still here. I'll admit, I haven't a clue how Henderson brought me back from the dead, but he managed it, and I'm here now. I'm exhausted, my chest is on fire, but considering I was officially dead, I'm not feeling too bad.'

'Did you see a bright light?' Will asked, lightening the mood. That meant she was off the hook - for now, at least.

'No. I felt a thud when I hit the ground, and that was it. No spiritual experiences, I'm afraid. If that's what a quick death is like, it's not so bad. I don't recommend trying it out for yourself, though.'

There was a knock at the door. It was Olli.

'Hi, mum, sorry to disturb you; I thought you might like some time alone.'

He was a good kid. She felt so thankful for her family. An overwhelming sensation of gratitude rushed over Charlotte, engulfing her. She was so pleased to be with them still. She began to cry.

'I'm sorry,' she apologised, 'It's all been a bit much for me.'

'It's just a quick one, Mum, then I'll leave you to rest.'

'It's fine, Olli, just ignore me. What is it?'

'I've sorted out the rotas with Isla, Piper and Agnieszka, so you don't have to worry about the kitchens for another week. We have no new bookings coming in, it's the documentary crew and Milo for the next five days—'

'Milo extended his stay?' Charlotte asked.

'Yes, he wants to stay around a little longer. Me, Willow and Lucia are heading into town with him this evening. He seems like a decent guy.'

Charlotte knew one of the reasons Milo wanted to stay. She'd tell Will later, he'd taken enough onboard for the time being. Besides, she owed Milo. She thought back to the incident at Saltburn, and she flashed back to how her foot had jammed in the tracks. Her face burned as she thought about how that situation might have played out.

'I have to tell you something about Milo,' she said to Will. 'Don't let me forget.'

'I've figured it out already,' Will replied. 'I can see it in their body language. We have to let it go, Charlotte. She's an adult, and she knows her mind. Besides, that kid was brilliant when you were out cold at the fairground. I was like a headless chicken. If it wasn't for the kids, Henderson reckons we'd have lost you. If Lucia likes him, that's good enough for me.'

He was right. Milo had earned himself a *Get Out of Jail Free* card. She resolved to let him and Lucia get on with it. It would play out in its own time.

'Sorry guys, but I need to pass on this message, I promised I'd let you know.'

Charlotte saw the urgency on his face. Olli was usually a calm character, but this seemed pressing.

'What is it, Olli? Thanks for taking care of the rotas.'

'It's the documentary crew. They're getting concerned. They haven't seen Casey since last night. They're worried something might have happened to her.'

SIX

Morecambe, 1996

'So, how's the move to detective going?' Larry asked. 'Any progress yet?'

It was a great day to be out on foot, patrolling the seafront. The sun was shining, the breeze was gentle, and the townsfolk appeared to be in no mood for any trouble. It was just how Frank Allan liked it. He'd be home in time to see the kids after school, and they might even get to enjoy a home-cooked dinner instead of a microwave meal.

'Imminent was how the boss described it,' Frank replied. 'They've got some paperwork to shuffle, pens to push and red tape to wrestle. It's going ahead, though. Any day now. Will you still speak to me when I'm out of uniform?'

'Yes, I reckon I might just manage it,' Larry replied. 'I'm going to miss you on the beat, though. I know you've always got my back. Can't say the same for these university-educated guys who swan in at brass level and haven't done the basics.'

It was time to change the subject. Larry had tried his hand at the Sergeant's exam several times. He'd become resentful of late, aware that he'd probably never move beyond constable level. The graduates were the target of his resentment.

'I'll miss this, too,' Frank replied. 'I like chatting to the residents and getting to know them. I'm worried that I won't get any of this contact with the public when I'm investigating cases. It'll be wall-to-wall villains for me—'

Frank held up his hand as a cyclist flew towards them on the pavement.

'You know it's illegal to be cycling on the pavement, son, don't you?'

It was a young man riding a mountain bike, a rucksack on his back. He looked like he was returning from a night shift.

'Yeah, sorry, Officer, I just wanted to get home. I'm knackered.'

'Fair enough, son, but use the road if you would. It might be your granny you crash into next time.'

The man nodded and moved his bike onto the road. He cycled off. Frank walked back over to Larry.

'Cheeky bastard's back on the pavement again,' Larry said, looking up the road.

'Well, that's just how it is,' Frank replied. 'But it doesn't mean we can't do our best to change their behaviour. Even if they ignore us.'

The two men continued walking and talking, Frank ever alert to the crackling of his radio.

'Yes, I'll miss this,' he continued, 'but I need something steadier for the sake of the kids. They're growing up; Kate will be moving on soon. I feel like we barely see each other, what with my shifts.'

'How are the kids?' Larry asked, nodding to a passer-by who appeared to know him from his civilian life. 'I mean, how are they after losing their mum like that?'

'Resilient is the word,' Frank answered. 'Imagine having to deal with that at their age. It's a lot to go through.'

He thought back to Evie's final days. It was still too raw for him; he blanked it out of his mind.

'I feel so guilty, but coming back to work helped me deal with it better. My mind was occupied by the job, I couldn't think about Evie. Sometimes I wonder if I rushed back too soon.'

Larry steered them into one of the resort's many arcades. The beeps and buzzes of the machines filled the air, along with the sound of falling coins and lively chatter.

'Does your Kate have any idea what she wants to do yet?' Larry asked.

'I think her mother dying has thrown her off course a bit,' Frank replied. 'I worry that she feels like she has to stay in Morecambe and look after me and Brett. She should be heading off for university or doing something fun with her life. I hope she doesn't feel obligated; I'd hate that.'

'You don't ever wish they'd follow you into the force?' Larry asked.

Frank always wondered if Larry would have liked a family of his own. It had never worked out that way for him. Instead, he'd always wanted to know about the kids and what plans they had for their future. It didn't bother Frank, it let him get his worries off his chest.

'You know, I'd be really proud if my Kate ever ended up in the police force. Not as a bobby, mind, but as a detective, maybe even brass. She's a bright kid and a hard worker. I've left it too late in my life to move up the ranks; I'm not made for it. But Kate could go somewhere, I reckon. I wouldn't dream of pressuring her, though. It would have to be her decision.'

'Excuse me, madam, you just dropped a coin,' Larry said, bending down to pick it up. He handed it to an old lady who'd just had a win on the slot machines.

'Thank you, Officer. I've only just won and already I'm throwing my cash around like I've got money to burn.'

The two men exchanged some chit-chat, made sure the lady had time to secure her winnings in her handbag, then moved on.

'And, what about Brett?' Larry continued. 'He must be a young man by now. How's he doing?'

'Not so well,' Frank replied, frowning. 'I'm worried about Brett. I know Kate will make something of her life. But Brett. He's a different creature.'

They'd reached the far end of the arcade and were exiting at the Festival Market end.

'He's more reckless and less responsible than Kate,' Frank continued. 'Goodness only knows what would happen if I weren't around; I think Brett might turn into a bit of a handful.'

They headed towards the Festival Market which was only just starting to get busy.

'That's why I've got to see this detective thing through. My days of dealing with the bad guys on the streets are numbered. I've got to look out for the kids now and think of their future. Life can be too hazardous on the beat. I've got to put myself out of harm's way behind a nice, safe desk.'

SEVEN

Charlotte woke with a jolt in the depths of the night. She was alone in bed; Will had opted to sleep on the sofa to give her the space she needed to recover.

'All you want now is my snoring to send you into a relapse,' he'd joked. At least they'd reached that stage of her near-death experience; the part where everybody felt it was safe enough to make jokes because they were confident she was going to make it.

Whatever Doctor Henderson had given her was doing the trick. Not only did she feel like she'd got her energy back, but it had also been providing a crazy dream world for her. Charlotte couldn't remember the last time she'd dreamt that vividly.

It took her a while to recall where she was and what had been going on. She was in the bedroom, alone, and Henderson's machine was still monitoring her various vital signs. He'd told them what to look for and warned Will to call him if it hit any dangerous ranges. Everything seemed steady to Charlotte. Besides, she felt good. Surely that was the best test.

The screen on her mobile phone faded to black. That usually meant a notification had just come in. The phone was on charge at the side of the bed, sharing a double socket with Henderson's medical equipment. Charlotte had discovered he kept a range of such devices in a storage container at the back of his garage. It made a change from old bikes and broken lawnmowers.

She picked up the phone and activated the screen. There was a text from Kate.

Josh has a holiday home at Golden Beaches Holiday Park! Going there at 9 am tomorrow. Wish you could come.

Golden Beaches Holiday Park was a caravan park in Heysham. Surely, that was playing with fire? She texted Kate.

I'm coming. Meet me at the Town Hall at 8.45? I'll be sneaking out! (I'm fine, honest)

There was a notification too, which was unfamiliar at first. Then she realised it was the new CCTV system. She opened the video file which had been uploaded to the CCTV monitoring service and watched it through. It appeared to be a misfire at first, but on second viewing, she thought she caught a glimpse of someone coming through the front entrance. Could it be Casey?

Charlotte felt awake and energised and was already weary of being confined to bed. Henderson had warned her about pushing herself too far but reckoned it was fine for her to be walking around at a gentle pace. She peeled off the adhesive tabs which were fastening the monitoring wires to her body and left them neatly piled on the sheets.

Charlotte climbed out of bed, unplugged her phone, and pulled on her dressing gown. She ran an inventory check on her battered body. Her mild burns were healing nicely, the various cuts and bruises were doing the same.

Her chest felt tight and sore, but she could tell that the drugs were helping with that. The discomfort was at a level she could cope with. Her brain was foggy, but she figured that was due to being laid out for so long. A bit of mental stimulation would soon clear that.

Creeping as quietly as she was able to, Charlotte headed for the door. She paused on Will's side of the bed. Her pockets had been emptied when she'd been moved up to the bedroom to recover. She picked up her pass card for the guest bedrooms.

Slowly, carefully, Charlotte opened the bedroom door. She stepped across the landing of the family accommodation, pausing outside each of the bedrooms to listen for sounds of life. All she could hear was Will's snoring from the lounge. She checked her phone; it was just past two o'clock. Even the kids would be out cold at that time.

She stepped over to the door to the family accommodation and placed her hand on the handle. She opened the door with the same care that she might have given had it been booby-trapped, fearing a squeak or a creak on the floorboards could give her away at any moment. If Will knew what she was up to, there would be a scene and an inquisition to deal with.

The door hinge creaked. She held the door partially open, unsure whether to continue or to cut her losses. She listened. There was no movement from any family members, so she carried on. She squeezed through a narrow gap, not daring to open the door fully. She made it, and the door obliged her by not making a sound again when she closed it behind her.

The guest house was completely quiet, as she'd expect it to be so late at night. Often, the rumble of TV sets could be heard until midnight or thereabouts, but the majority of the guests tended to settle down by that time.

Casey's room was on the second floor. Charlotte was less cautious walking down the staircase. Nobody else would care much who was creeping about at that time of night. She paused outside Casey's room, listening for signs of life. Will and the kids had last seen Casey when she'd lost her contact lens on the night of her accident. They'd never found the lens, and Will reported her being quite upset by that.

There was no sound from within the room, so Charlotte decided to take a small risk. She texted Casey, thanking her lucky stars that they'd exchanged numbers to coordinate their ill-fated night out. She shuddered as she recalled how close she'd come to getting hurt that evening at the hands of the three men.

Charlotte wrote a brief text.

Are you okay, Casey?

She pressed send.

She heard a notification sound through the door, then saw on her screen that the message had been delivered. Was Casey in there? Had that been her setting off the CCTV alert earlier?

Charlotte sent another text.

I'm outside your door. Can I come in? We're worried about you.

Once again, she heard a notification sound in Casey's room. The message showed as being delivered, but there was no reply.

Casey was a grown woman, and a paying guest, too. She had every right to do as she pleased while staying in the hotel. She had a key card; it was a place to stay, not a prison. But something wasn't sitting right with Charlotte. She dialled Casey's phone this time. There was a slight delay, then she heard Casey's phone ringing in her room. She let it ring ten times, then ended the call. Surely, she'd have answered it, even if she had company?

Charlotte texted a final time.

I'm coming into your room to check you're okay. Shout if you're in there!

She waited a short time, long enough to get a reply to the delivered message, then took her key card from her dressing gown pocket and opened the door. She pushed it open cautiously, whispering Casey's name.

'Casey? Casey? It's me, Charlotte. Is it okay to come in?'

There was no reply. Charlotte opened the door fully and walked into the room. The room was made up, but the bed was undisturbed. Casey's suitcase was open at the side of her bed and there was an array of filming equipment neatly arranged by the window. The curtains were open. At the side of the bed was a book, half-read, by an author Charlotte had never heard of before. His name was Bradley Webster.

She looked around the bedroom for signs that Casey had been there. Her phone was on charge at the side of the bed. The screen was unlocked, and she could see that many messages were waiting to be looked at, as well as her own. Everything looked like Casey had just gone out for the day, except for her phone. Why had she left that behind?

Charlotte walked into the ensuite bathroom and switched on the light. The bathroom was neat and orderly, except for the sink, which was surrounded by the usual items: hairbrush, deodorant, toothbrush and toothpaste, as well as some loose hair clips, a couple of hair bands and some sanitary products. But perched on the sink was a contact lens holder, still open, with a single lens perched in one of the cradles. To the side was a cleaning solution. But, it was what Casey had left on the top of the toilet cistern which gave Charlotte a jolt. Sitting there, in an open glasses case, was a pair of spectacles. Set within the frame were the thickest lenses she had ever seen.

EIGHT

Casey's name was written in the glasses case in a childish hand: *Gogs*. That was the name of the girl in the photo, the one that Val and the woman with the video had talked about. She'd been wearing thick lenses in the photographs. She was known as Goggles and Gogs; Casey Gogarty and Gogs had to be one and the same person.

Charlotte wished Casey was with her at that moment so she could seek confirmation. She'd been right under their noses all the time. It had to be her, it was too big a coincidence. She took her phone out of her pocket and texted Kate.

'Please be awake still,' she said to herself.

Casey is Gogs/Goggles! I'm sure of it!

She took a photo of the spectacles in the glasses case and added it to the text message. She waited to make sure the message had been delivered. Moments later, Kate got back to her.

You're supposed to be ill! Is Casey there? Have you asked?

Charlotte almost jumped with joy when Kate got back

to her. She wasn't certain she could hang onto this new information until morning.

Casey is missing! Her team hasn't seen her. You don't think???

Her heart jumped at the thought of it. At least that meant Henderson was doing something right. Was Casey caught up in whatever was going on?

FFS. You don't think she's in danger, do you? Can I call you?

Kate's reply came fast.

Don't ring! In bed with hubby :-) Trying not to disturb him with my dead of night texting. Will pick you up at Town Hall tomorrow. Don't come if you're too ill!!!!!!

Charlotte was wide awake. She wanted company. How could she hang onto information like that all night? There were another six hours to pass until she saw Kate, and she was certain she wasn't going to be able to get back to sleep.

Casey's phone was still on the bedside table. There might be clues on there. She unplugged it from the charger and activated the screen, navigating directly to the text messages. She ignored her messages and scrolled through the various texts from her documentary team.

You okay hun? Missed you at dinner. Let us know where you are. x

I have your contact lens. Found it on the dining room floor. Let me know when you're back, will drop it off in your room.

It was nice to see her colleagues looking out for her. If Charlotte had to describe the scene in Casey's room, she'd have said it looked like Casey had just been going about her regular business. Only, something had disturbed her. She scrolled back further in the messages. Will had told her about Casey's missing lens, so it must have happened close to the time they were due to meet at the funfair.

There they were. Three texts had been sent at about the time she'd seen the mystery man getting off his motorbike close to the funfair.

I'll meet you at the end of the stone jetty at 7.30. See you then GOGS.

The man must have been getting ready to meet Casey when they'd been at the funfair. Charlotte reckoned she must have disturbed him when he'd spotted her following him.

Delayed slightly. It'll be worth your while. Meet at Rita's on the other side of the road. 8pm.

Charlotte pictured where he'd parked his motorcycle. It was almost opposite Rita's, so he'd changed his plans. He must have been walking around that area while the cops were still there. The guy had some nerve, that was for sure.

Casey had been impatient by the time she received his third message.

WTF? Don't waste my time. 8pm or you can get lost, whoever you are.

She'd got her reply, just before 8 o' clock.

Patience, Goggles. Do you want to know what happened that night? I'm the only one who knows. Be there.

Charlotte slipped Casey's phone into her pocket. This was incredible. This man seemed to know everything. He even knew Casey was Goggles. Nobody had made that connection in the police investigation. Gogs and her family had moved away and that was the end of it. It had happened twenty-five years ago. So why was she back in Morecambe now, filming a documentary on the subject? And, more to the point, why hadn't she told Charlotte who she was?

Charlotte checked the time on her phone. It wasn't even

three o'clock yet. There was nothing she could do until morning.

She took a last look around Casey's room to see if there were any more clues as to her whereabouts. There was nothing. She wondered how much Casey could see without her lenses; was she short or long-sighted?

Charlotte walked back into the bathroom and picked up the spectacles. They were heavy; the frames were also too small for her to wear. She held them in front of her eyes and looked in the mirror. Not only could she barely see anything, but it also made her eyeballs seem enlarged and almost comedic. This had to be an old pair of glasses; there was no way a woman like Casey would wear these. They were probably her childhood spectacles.

Charlotte placed them back in the case and walked out into Casey's room. She examined Casey's open suitcase. She'd missed it the first time, but there was a second spectacles case perched on top of a sweater. She opened it up, but the case was empty. Charlotte knew enough about contact lenses to know most wearers kept a spare pair of glasses, in case of infection, loss or discomfort. That must account for the second empty box.

Her mind was buzzing with possibilities and explanations; she wanted the new day to start right there. But, Doctor Henderson had been stern in his warnings, ordering her to rest until he was certain that she had recovered sufficiently. Charlotte couldn't wait that long, and she had a plan to join Kate when she paid her visit to Josh Irving.

Charlotte crept out of Casey's room and back up the staircase to the family accommodation. She opened the door once again, pausing when it creaked at the same position. She returned to her bedroom and listened for a few moments to make sure she hadn't disturbed the family.

Then, removing her dressing gown and taking her jeans off the back of the chair, she set about creating a body-sized shape underneath the bedclothes. The chances were, her family would be sleeping in until late, enabling her to sneak out to join Kate for her early-morning visit. But, just to be certain, she was going to make it look like she was still asleep in there, just in case someone did check in on her.

NINE

It couldn't have been a better day to be assigned a police vehicle. The weather had been foul all week and pounding the streets of Morecambe on foot was not the most attractive prospect. As Frank re-arranged his belongings in his locker, he paused a moment to look at the photo of Brett and Kate that was pinned to the inside. He'd soon be clear of these shifts and on a more normal schedule. All week, he'd missed meeting them home from school. He felt guilty as hell, but what could he do? Somebody had to put the food on the table. He thanked his lucky stars for Kate.

'Who's driving?' Larry asked as he slammed his locker shut and turned the key.

'Go on, you pick up the keys,' Frank smiled. Larry was like a kid in a toy shop whenever they were assigned to a task that needed a police vehicle. He lived for the moment when the blue lights went on, and he got to use his advanced driver training skills on the resort's roads.

'You've been watching too many Starsky and Hutch re-runs on the television,' Frank teased him. 'I don't think we're likely to be carrying out too many high-speed chases today.'

Their task was simple, and it allowed Frank to speak to his detective colleagues on a separate floor. Somebody was stealing motorcycles from the resort and selling them on in Liverpool. That was what the detectives were investigating. For Frank and Larry, their primary task of the day was to visit various trouble hot spots where teenagers had been spotted riding bikes on public land. Their job was to enforce the law, but if they found a useful lead to pass on to the investigating team, then all the better.

Where Larry was content to play cops and robbers, Frank had his eye on the bigger prize. If he could provide a strong lead, or even an arrest, in the motorcycle thefts opera-tion, it could help to accelerate his move to Detective Constable.

'Where to first?' Larry asked as they opened up the vehicle that had been assigned to them for the day. 'How about we start at Heysham Moss and head back?'

'Good call,' Frank replied. They'd been given a list of trouble spots around the area. The closer they got to the schools finishing for the day, the more likely it was that they'd catch some teenage riders red-handed.

The car radio crackled into life.

'Damn, I've only just started the engine,' Larry cursed. 'What do they want with us already? I was looking forward to a nice, easy day today.'

'Control to CH 14,' came the voice from the control room.

'CH14 uncommitted, go ahead,' Frank answered, shrugging at Larry.

'CH14 report of children in boarded-up property on Thornton Road. Can you attend?'

'We've been there before,' Larry remarked, 'I wish the owner would just board it up properly. Those school kids are a pain in the arse.'

'CH14 en route, I know the address' Frank replied, then replaced the radio in its holder.

'It won't take too long,' he tried to reassure Larry. 'Besides, the schools aren't even finished for the day yet. It'll increase our chances of catching someone in the act when we get to Heysham.'

Frank fastened his seatbelt and Larry released the handbrake. There was a knock at Frank's window, and he held up his hand for Larry not to move the car. He wound his window down. Constable Pickering bent down so that she was level with Frank.

'So, you two bastards got the cushy deal today. Don't worry about us poor sods who have to pound the beat in this shitty weather.'

Frank smiled at her. Pickering was also hoping to become a detective any time soon; they often compared notes about the transfer process.

'Any word yet?' Frank asked.

'Bugger all,' Pickering replied. 'Looks like you and me will be wearing out more boots before they move us to a desk job. They keep telling me, 'soon', but the brass is in no hurry, that's for sure.'

'We'll get there,' Frank tried to reassure her, but he wasn't so certain himself.

Pickering waved them off in the car.

'Try not to stay too dry, you jammy bastards,' she called after them as Larry reversed out of the parking space.

'She's sharp, is Amanda,' Frank remarked, as he gave her

a wave. 'It wouldn't surprise me if she made DCI or Super-intendent one day; she's got what it takes.'

'If I didn't know you better, I'd say you two have a thing going,' Larry teased. 'I can see the sparks when she talks to you. I reckon you'd be in there if you made more of an effort.'

'Come on, Larry,' Frank sighed. 'I'm not ready to think about that. Besides, I have the kids. They're still adjusting to life without their mother. I like Amanda, but I can't even go there just yet. I have to put Brett and Kate first.'

They drove on, out to the seafront and along the prome-nade. Frank thought about Amanda in silence. They'd always been pals, but it was too soon. Maybe later, once the kids were more settled.

Larry pulled up directly outside the boarded-up house. It was three-storeys high and one of a small row of terraces on a residential street just off the promenade.

'They can't find the owner, how the hell does a property like this fall into such disrepair?' Frank asked.

'I'll bet the locals love having an eyesore like that on the street,' Larry replied, switching off the engine and reaching to the back of the car for his helmet.

'CH14 to Control,' Frank spoke into the radio.

'Go ahead, CH14,' came the reply.

'CH14 on the scene at Thornton Road.'

'Thank you, CH14.'

'Right, let's see what the little tykes are up to,' Larry said, climbing out of the car.

The ground floor windows of the property were boarded up with low-grade chipboard which was struggling to cope with the onslaught of wind and rain coming in off the bay. It was hanging away from the window frames, and a large area had been broken at the bottom of the front window.

'There's going to be an accident in this building soon,' an old man said, as he stepped out of his front door to speak to the officers. 'It's causing no end of trouble. Can't the council come and get it boarded up properly?'

Frank and Larry said a few words to reassure the man, then headed around the back, where they knew the youngsters would have made their entry. The gate to the rear of the terrace was reached via a narrow lane off Dallam Avenue. It was the perfect place for truants to lurk, backing directly onto the fields to the school. The back gate was rotten and falling off its hinges, the yard overgrown and abandoned. Since Frank had last checked over the property, the chipboard on the kitchen window had been pulled away from the frame and was now lying on the ground, rotting. The glass was broken, and one of the side windows swung open in the frame. The kids had even placed a metal dustbin upside down so that they could climb inside and come and go as they pleased.

'I'll bet the little buggers saw us coming and ran off,' Larry said, as he weighed up the climb they were about to make.

Frank took the lead, using what was left of an iron pipe to haul himself up and climb onto the bin, then pulling himself through the window cautiously, mindful of some shattered glass on the windowsill inside.

'I don't know how this building is still standing,' he remarked to Larry, who was struggling to pull himself up onto the dustbin.

Frank scanned the kitchen. It was a wreck. Old-fashioned wallpaper was hanging off the walls. Plaster was coming loose and falling away where the property had become particularly damp. Slogans and nicknames were sprayed all over the walls. There were lager and beer cans strewn all over, as well as cigarette stubs and discarded matches.

Larry finally succeeded in getting through the window and climbed down into the kitchen, out of breath. The two men walked through into the dining room and lounge, which had been knocked through.

What was left of a wet, decaying carpet that lined the floor, was littered with food debris, drink cans, and cigarette ends.

'Hello. Anybody here?' Frank shouted.

'I think they've done a runner,' Larry suggested.

There was a creak from a floorboard in the room above them.

Frank pointed upward and indicated with his hand that he was heading for the hallway. He started to move up the staircase, which creaked and groaned as if it had almost given up on life. It was impossible to make a quiet entrance, so he called up the staircase.

'Morecambe Police. Come on kids, this building is not safe. You need to get yourselves back to school.'

He heard giggling, then a voice that was half broken from within one of the upstairs bedrooms.

'Fuck off, pigs!'

Frank ran up the staircase, calling for Larry to join him.

By the time Frank reached the room where the voice had come from, it was empty. He looked out the window to see two figures in school uniform making their way out the back gate. Larry walked into the room, puffing from running up the stairs.

'The little buggers climbed down next door's drainpipe and onto the flat roof,' Frank remarked, after peering out of the window. 'So now I guess we know there's an escape route out the back of this place.'

TEN

Charlotte thrust her hand under the sheet and shuffled her jeans around to make the shape more convincing. She couldn't believe she was resorting to schoolboy capers to sneak out of the house. The chances were she'd be back by ten o'clock, and nobody would even know she'd been gone. But just in case, if anybody looked in on her, a cursory glance would make it appear that she was still in bed and fast asleep. As for the monitoring machine, it was easily silenced by switching it off at the socket.

Having made her exit out of the family accommodation once, Charlotte was now wise to the creak in the door. By twenty minutes to nine, she'd managed to creep down the stairs, avoid the documentary crew and Isla, and sneak out of the back door. As Kate pulled up at the side of the road to pick her up, she shook her head.

'I didn't expect to see you here,' Kate said as Charlotte climbed into the passenger seat at her side. 'How are you even on your feet already?'

'It's all thanks to a fine cocktail of drugs provided by Doctor Henderson,' Charlotte answered, putting her hand out to grab the seatbelt clip. She winced as a sharp pain shot through her chest.

'Oh, Jesus Christ!' she shouted out.

'Charlotte, you shouldn't be here. I'm running you back to the guest house. You need to be in bed.'

'I'm fine, I'm not having a heart attack or anything like that. The doctor said I've got a strong heart; it's not as if I'm some middle-aged man with a dicky ticker. It was the electric shock that caused my problem, not my heart. I'll be good to go in no time.'

Kate looked at her, a combination of despair and resignation in her eyes.

'If you die on the job, I'll never hear the end of it,' she continued. 'Promise me, if you think you're going to keel over, you'll let me know so I can drop you off at the roadside and pretend I'm not involved.'

'I promise,' Charlotte smiled, making a second attempt at the seat belt.

'Here,' Kate said, unclipping her belt and reaching across Charlotte to help.

'Besides,' Charlotte continued, 'it's the compressions that made my chest sore, not my heart stopping. The doctor told me he's broken ribs before when he does compressions. No wonder it hurts so much—'

She secured her seatbelt.

'The drugs are taking care of everything else,' Charlotte added. 'You have my permission to roll me into a ditch and run away if I die on you. You have my personal guarantee that I won't land you with the paperwork. How's that for a good friend?'

Kate pulled away from the kerb.

'I'd prefer it if you didn't die on me,' she said, checking her wing mirror. 'What did Will say when he found out you were coming with me this morning?'

Charlotte said nothing.

'Charlotte?'

'He's still in bed—' she began.

'You mean he doesn't know,' Kate scolded. 'Damn, Charlotte, you don't make it easy to stay out of trouble. We'll visit Josh, then you're going straight home.'

Charlotte ran a quick body check. The truth was, she felt okay. She'd done a bit of internet research while she was waiting for dawn to arrive, and she'd ascertained that she was lucky to be alive. But, as Henderson had told her, most people who ended up on a defibrillator had bad hearts to start with, so they were already in a bad state when their hearts gave out. It was the electric shock that had screwed things up for her. He'd jump-started her with a cocktail of compressions, defibrillator, drugs and adrenaline, and - thank God - it had done the job. She was ready to get back to the action.

'I will take it easy, I promise,' she said in a final attempt to reassure her friend. 'But I can't see the harm in gentle house visits. I won't be doing any running around or anything like that. I reckon sedentary activities like visiting Josh will be good for me.'

'Okay, I don't believe you for one minute, but I'm stuck with you now, Charlotte. Talk me through what you found in Casey's room. Do I need to send a couple of officers round to check it over?'

'There was no sign of a struggle; it looked like she'd gone to meet this chap on the seafront. I've got her phone with me. Here, I'll put it on your dashboard—'

Charlotte slid Casey's phone out of her back pocket and placed it to the side of Kate.

'She doesn't lock it, and I left it fully charged, so you

won't have any problem accessing her text messages. I didn't delve any deeper than that; I figure Casey's entitled to her privacy. I'll leave the snooping to you guys.'

Charlotte hadn't been concentrating on the journey, but she looked up and saw that they were heading out toward Heysham now.

'Are we certain Casey is missing?' Kate asked. 'I mean, we have to allow for her meeting someone and staying overnight. We don't want to have every patrol car in More-cambe looking out for her when she's doing the walk of shame. The poor woman is entitled to a private life.'

'But, you'll want to speak to her anyway, won't you? I mean, she's Gogs, the girl that everybody's been talking about. Nobody knew what happened to her, and, there she is, a guest in one of my rooms. Why didn't she tell me? Why did she meet that guy who's been trying to hurt me? She might be in danger—'

'Okay, you've convinced me,' Kate interrupted. 'As soon as we get to Golden Beaches Holiday Park, I'll call the office and issue an alert for Casey. We can't start a manhunt, but the patrol cars can keep an eye out for her, at least.'

'Good, thanks,' Charlotte said. 'I think that's the right thing. Besides, she can lead us to that guy.'

'When we speak to Josh, you need to leave me to ask the questions,' Kate said after a short silence. 'You're an observer only. I want to do the preliminary interview myself. I have DI Lowe meeting me there to accompany me in an official capacity. So, no journalism, okay? The DSU agreed to you tagging along again, but strictly speaking, I'm letting you attend this because you're a friend, and, despite everything, I trust you.'

'Thanks,' Charlotte replied. She appreciated what Kate was doing. The unique access would give her one hell of a story once the dust had settled, and all the details could finally be revealed.

'What's Josh's name now, by the way,' she added, realising that Kate hadn't yet filled her in with the details.

'He goes under the name of Bradley Webster these days —' Kate began.

'Jesus, Bradley Webster?' Charlotte exclaimed. 'Casey had one of his books by her bedside. She must be in this up to her neck.'

ELEVEN

Josh's holiday lodge was the up-market variety. It had a small garden, an excellent view of the bay, and a beautifully decorated decking area. It also appeared from the outside to be more of a bungalow than a temporary structure.

Kate and Charlotte left the car in the visitor's parking area, not wanting to attract attention at the caravan. DI Lowe was delayed in a traffic snarl-up on his way into work from Lancaster; he recommended that Kate start without him. The two women were sitting on a bench, giving themselves a vantage point from which to study Josh's holiday home unobserved.

'Sorry to sound like a school teacher, Charlotte, but we need to go through the ground rules again. You have to observe only. If he speaks to you or exchanges pleasantries, that's fine, but no formal questions about the case.'

'Understood,' Charlotte confirmed. 'I'll say nothing.'

'After DCI Comfort messed up so badly, it allowed DSU Pickering to get the Chief to put everything back as it was. Let's not screw it up again while the Police Commissioner has had her wings clipped.'

'Agreed,' Charlotte replied. 'He must be doing alright if this is a holiday home. What do you reckon that lodge is worth, sixty or seventy thousand pounds?'

'Who knows?' Kate answered. 'Let's go and find out.'

Kate took out her mobile phone and keyed in a text message.

'You've got your phone replaced,' Charlotte observed.

'Yes, with strict instructions not to wreck this one. Josh will open the door to us, and we'll just walk in now I've told him we're here. The deal is that nobody knows we're police. Okay, let's go.'

Charlotte felt her ribs protesting as she stood up. She was sluggish still; she couldn't be sure if that was the drugs or the bruising from Henderson's CPR. Despite the discomfort, Charlotte was still pleased to be doing something. She hated lying about in bed.

As they approached the front door, it opened up and a neatly dressed man let them in. Charlotte examined his face. She could see that this was the Josh Irving of the photographs in the way that Eric Bennett was not so cut-and-dried.

'Come in,' he said, holding out his hand to greet them.

Kate made the introductions and reiterated that Charlotte was only an observer.

'I've enjoyed your writing,' Josh said when he heard Charlotte's name. 'I live in Kent now, but I have The Bay View Weekly delivered on subscription. I've read your work. It's very good.'

Charlotte glanced at Kate, uncertain of what she was allowed to say.

'I'm very flattered,' she replied. 'I see you're a writer too.'

Josh motioned for them to take a seat. It was less of a

holiday lodge and more of a luxury bungalow. The finish and furnishings oozed quality and good taste. Charlotte hadn't realised they made models to such a high specification.

'Yes, writing has been very good to me,' Josh replied, heading over to the kitchen area in the open plan lounge. 'Drinks, ladies?'

As he boiled the kettle and prepared the hot drinks, he gave an unprompted overview of his life.

'I'm dyslexic, you know; it used to cause me no end of problems as a child. When I was in youth custody, I had a social worker who got me some help. I used to spend my time scribbling stories and reading books. Once I had some coping strategies in place, there was no stopping me. Ironically, writing books has provided excellent cover all these years. Nobody has a clue who I am, but I can make a living out of sight and out of mind. It's worked well for me.'

Josh put the drinks on a tray, emptied some chocolate biscuits onto a plate and walked over to Kate and Charlotte, placing the refreshments on the coffee table that was just in front of them.

'Thank you for agreeing to speak to us today—' Kate began.

'Well, it came as a bit of a shock,' Josh interrupted. 'My wife thinks I'm up here finishing a novel. It's required a level of subterfuge that I thought I'd put behind me.'

'I realise that you were contacted under exceptional circumstances,' Kate resumed, 'and we're extremely grateful for your assistance. We will, of course, preserve your anonymity, and I must stress from the outset that you are not a suspect in this case.'

'I'm glad to hear it,' Josh smiled. 'I think I've already had my punishment, don't you, DCI Summers?'

He was not at all what Charlotte had expected. She was desperate to ask questions, but set about the chocolate digestive biscuits instead to distract herself. He sounded so educated. She'd assumed him to be rough-and-ready from the conversations she'd had.

'I'm just going to ask some general questions,' Kate continued, 'and, I apologise if these cause you any distress or discomfort after all this time.'

'Okay, I've had fair warning, let's get this over with. I'm happy to help as this is a murder investigation, but you'll understand if I get this over with and return to Kent as soon as possible?'

Kate nodded.

'First, have you had any contact with any of the other children who were involved in Dave Brewer's death? Or your sister, Val?'

'No. I know my brother has been released from jail because I read the papers. I will admit to having watched my sister from a distance when I've been staying in the resort, but I have honoured the anonymity arrangement and never contacted her. That's probably been the cruellest part of this whole sorry affair.'

Kate had brought a notepad, in which she was making notes. She looked up once she'd finished scribbling.

'Have you received any contacts from anybody about the case? Either recently or in the past?'

'No, never. I did my time in youth custody, I got out, was given a new identity and I've made the most of it. I studied in evening classes, got my exams and went to university. I met my wife at university, and, except for my siblings, I got so caught up in my wonderful new life, I completely forgot about the past. When I look back now, it's like it never happened. I can barely believe it's true, sometimes.'

'Did you kill David Brewer?'

Josh looked at Kate as if he wasn't expecting a question as blunt as that.

'Our deal here, DCI Summers, is that I assist you with your ongoing investigation. I'm not here to rake over old coals.'

'My apologies,' Kate replied, shuffling on the seat. It was all Charlotte could do not to chip in.

'Is there anybody you can think of who might want revenge on your brother? We're trying to establish who might hold a grudge. Two people have died already, and several have been threatened or injured, including my colleague here—'

'You've been threatened?' Josh asked.

Charlotte nodded, reluctant to say more.

'I'm sorry,' he said, shaking his head. 'I thought we were done with this. We paid the price, Brewer was dead, it was over. I haven't a clue why this reared its ugly head again.'

'Was there a fifth person involved that night?' Kate ventured. Charlotte knew she was playing with fire. 'Was a girl called Casey Gogarty caught up in what happened that night?'

Josh stood up.

'Enough!' he said. He turned his back to Kate and Charlotte and looked out the window, which gave an incredible view over the bay.

'You're not investigating what happened twenty-five years ago. You're supposed to be asking me about the present day—'

'But it has a bearing on what's happening now—'

'I haven't seen Gogs for over twenty-five years. If you'd have asked me, I wouldn't even have been able to tell you her name until you mentioned it. She was just Goggles or Gogs to us, we never used her name. I don't know what happened to her.'

Kate was silent while she waited for Josh to calm and settle. At last, he returned to his armchair.

'Look, Officer, I'm not sure I can help you. This has been over for me for years. I have a new life, a new identity, a wife and a family. It's like a bad dream. I have this holiday accommodation because this was my home, my roots are here. I have to wander this resort like a ghost, and I'll admit that I have watched my sister from afar, just to make sure she's okay. Every part of me wants to see my brother, Seth, again, but I know that can't ever happen—'

He paused a moment, then took a deep breath.

'My wife doesn't even know about my past, DCI Summers. I accepted a long time ago that it's a secret I have to take to my grave. If I was ever connected with what happened twenty-five years ago, it would blow my life apart. There's not a day that goes by that I don't want to see my brother, to reach out and help him. But this is a pretence I have to maintain, Officer. If I ever let the veil slip, my life will be over.'

TWELVE

Morecambe, 1996

'Well, I won't be climbing down the drainpipe to chase them,' Larry laughed. 'I'm not sure it would take my weight.'

'Yes, we're too old for that,' Frank agreed. 'We'll pop round to the school and give them an update. The sooner something is done with this old house, the better. It's an accident waiting to happen. Imagine living next door to it?'

Frank and Larry checked the remaining rooms, then made their way back to the kitchen window to let themselves out. The entire property was a wreck, with rising damp, peeling wallpaper, worn and dangerous carpets, and the debris left by teenagers, tramps, druggies and anybody else for whom such a hideaway was a desirable place.

Having checked in with the headteacher at the school and brought him up to speed, the two police officers were clear to resume their task of monitoring for illegal bikers at the resort's trouble spots.

'At least the schools are finished for the day now,' Frank said as Larry parked the car at Meldon Road. 'This is the best time to catch them at it.'

They stepped out of the car and began the walk along the narrow track, and over the railway bridge.

'I don't hear any engines,' Larry remarked, as he held back a bramble to allow Frank to pass without snagging his uniform.

A middle-aged couple walking a couple of Cairn Terriers waved from further along the path and began to make their way towards them as if they had something to share.

'Good afternoon, officers,' the man said, 'or should I say good evening now the nights are drawing in already?'

'I hope you're here for the bikers?' the woman added. 'They're a - excuse my language, officers - a bloody nuisance. I almost got knocked down by one the other day. He roared out the bushes from nowhere. It gave me the fright of my life.'

'There's an old motorbike hidden in that bush,' the man continued, pointing. 'I don't know if it will give you any clues. It's only been there a day or two; it looks like one of the kids has hidden it.'

Frank thanked the couple for their help, then walked over to the bush where the motorcycle was supposed to be hidden. Sure enough, poorly concealed under a tarpaulin and covered with branches, was a mud-covered bike. Its tyres were bald, and it had fragments of branches and bushes caught in its engine and spokes.

'I'll radio this in,' Frank suggested. 'It's going to need a recovery team to get this back to the station. With any luck, the chassis number will give us a clue as to what's happening to all these bikes.'

They returned to the car, and Frank radioed in the location and details of their find. It was a good haul for Frank; it would remind the brass that he was still angling for that detective's position.

'Whinnysty Lane next?' Larry asked. 'We can pick up a chocolate bar at the shops while we're there?'

Larry drove them back toward the resort, and they parked up at the road end, facing out toward the bay. As with the Moss, there was no sound of engines to greet them as they stepped out of the car. There was one more car parked there, where an elderly couple were coaxing their animals into the rear of the vehicle.

'The little buggers are never around when you want them,' Larry grumbled. 'I'm sure these kids can smell us from a mile off.'

To their left was a patch of grass that had been chewed up by motorcycle tyres. A row of expensive properties overlooked the grass strip; it wasn't difficult to see why the residents were so agitated by the motorcycling problem.

'I'll see if this couple can tell us anything,' Larry said, as he walked toward the second car and started chatting with them. Frank looked out across the grassed area, then admired the view of the bay. His attention was caught by the sound of a single motorcycle behind him. He turned around to see what was heading their way. He gave Larry a wave to show that he'd handle it.

Frank noticed the rider's body language change as he came over the rise in the road to be greeted by the sight of two police officers. His cop's antennae fired at once. The rider brought the bike to a stop and got off it in the most deliberate way possible. If he'd been taking his motorcycle test, he couldn't have been more cautious.

Frank walked over, introduced himself and explained

that he'd be asking some routine questions. As the rider lifted his visor, Frank could see it was a young kid; it was borderline if he was even the legal age to ride the bike. He hadn't bolted, so Frank assumed he had nothing to hide.

There was something about this youth that was familiar to Frank. As he asked to see his licence, Frank finally realised who it was. He recognised him as one of Jonny Irving's kids. He'd answered the door to them the night they'd brought their drunk father home.

It had bothered Frank, seeing those three kids like that. If ever there was a case for social services to get more involved, that was probably it. But Frank knew only too well, families were fragile things and life could turn sour in an instant.

With Larry preoccupied by fussing over the couple's dogs, Frank made the snap decision to let the kid off with a warning. He was polite and contrite and didn't seem to be a trouble-maker. Besides, if there was anything he'd learned as a beat copper in the resort, it was that you picked your battles. Letting Jonny Irving's boy off like that might make the difference between him viewing the local cops as a friend or the enemy. Those kids had enough to tolerate with their father; he had no intention of adding to the family's woes that day.

'We'll be patrolling this area over the next couple of weeks,' Frank warned him as he prepared to ride off. 'Give it a miss for a while, eh? I don't want you landing yourself in trouble,' he cautioned.

Larry finished his conversation with the dog walkers and re-joined Frank at the car.

'Who was the kid?' Larry asked. 'He looked like he was up to no good.'

'It was nobody, Larry,' Frank replied, looking at Irving's boy as he disappeared over the rise in the road. 'I doubt we'll even see the kid again; he doesn't seem to be the trouble-making kind.'

THIRTEEN

Charlotte's phone vibrated in her pocket, and she drew it out as subtly as she could; she did not want to appear rude. It was a text from Nigel.

Jon Rogers has been in touch from Morecambe Library. He's asking if you can go in. Haven't heard from you. Is everything okay?

There was no way Nigel could have known what she'd been through since they'd last chatted. She would have to bring him up to speed, and she wanted to do that face-to-face. After they'd finished with Josh, she'd get Kate to drop her off at the office. The library was within easy walking distance, and she'd catch a taxi back to the guest house. That way she wouldn't place herself under too much physical strain.

Kate took the cue to check her phone.

'Excuse me for one moment,' she apologised to Josh. She read her texts and dialled into her voicemail.

'DI Lowe won't be joining us now,' she said, 'The traffic is backed up with an accident. He sends his apologies.'

'No problem,' Josh replied, 'I think we're almost done here, aren't we?'

Kate ignored his last comment and continued with her update.

'We've got a lead on your man's motorcycle, Charlotte. Are you up to a trip to White Lund Industrial Estate before I drop you off home?'

Charlotte shuddered as she thought back to the industrial unit where Vinnie Mace had threatened to torture her and Will. It was a good job the cash and carry was based there, or there was a good chance neither of them would have returned to the industrial estate ever again after that experience.

'Where are we going?' she asked.

'Baker's Breakers,' Kate answered. 'It's a scrapyard. The owner reported a scrap motorcycle had gone missing. It fits the description of the one your assailant was using—'

'Assailant?' Josh remarked. 'What on earth has been going on around here?'

'It's a long story, but we would not have sought permission to speak to you if we didn't think it was important.'

Kate looked him directly in the eyes. They'd got off to a shaky start, but there were signs Josh might be coming round.

'Look, I want to help, Officer, really I do. I'm just not sure how I can.'

There was a thump from the back of Josh's lodge.

'What was that?' Kate asked.

'Oh, it'll be nothing, probably just a book falling off my bed.'

Josh dismissed it a little too fast, and Charlotte could see that Kate had clocked it too.

'You don't want to go and check?'

'It's fine, it's nothing,' Josh reiterated. 'Do you have any more questions to ask me before you're on your way, Detective?'

Kate waited a moment before answering. Charlotte knew her friend well; she would not want to leave without asking about her father.

'May I ask you a question that's not related to the Brewer murder?' she ventured. 'It's about my father who was killed shortly before your own case. I think it was a few days before, yet it was never linked with Dave Brewer's death.'

'Sure,' Josh replied, looking over towards the door to the hallway. 'You can try your luck, but don't get your hopes up.'

'Did you know my father? He was PC Frank Allan. He was stabbed and shot shortly before David Brewer died—'

Josh stood up.

'If you don't mind, I will check if that noise was anything to worry about. These lodges creak and groan a bit at times; they don't have foundations like a regular house. I'll be back with you in a moment.'

Josh walked over to the door, partially opened it, walked through, then closed it behind him.

'Now that's suspicious,' Kate whispered.

'He's not being particularly helpful, is he?' Charlotte remarked.

Kate nodded.

'I have to be careful as he's not a suspect in the case. I mean, it's obvious he's not the guy who chased you on the e-scooter or threw the electrical cable at you. But, he can withdraw his cooperation at any time, all the time he's not implicated in our ongoing investigation. I can't help feeling he's not telling us everything—'

'Listen,' Charlotte interrupted. 'He's talking to someone.'

Kate was silent. She got up and moved toward the hallway door.

'He might be on the phone,' she suggested.

'I'll bet there's someone in the back,' Charlotte ventured.

'We can't push it because he's not a suspect. I can't search the house or even make any veiled threats. If I do, he might withdraw his support entirely. I daren't risk that.'

'He's coming!' Charlotte warned.

Kate darted back to the sofa, and Charlotte took a biscuit to make it look natural when Josh returned.

He walked through the door, looking a little flustered.

'Is everything alright?' Kate asked.

'Yes, yes — it was my shower gel falling off the hook, that's all—'

'Only, it sounded like you were speaking to somebody—'

'Oh, you heard that? It was just my - er - it was just my editor updating me about something on my phone. I had him on speakerphone. Are we done now?'

Kate gave Charlotte a momentary glance.

'Almost done,' Kate resumed. 'Just that matter of PC Frank Allan.'

'He was your father, you say?' Josh asked.

'Yes. I was a teenager when he died.'

'I'm sorry to hear that. Really, I am sorry. I knew your father, but only as a local bobby. He was one of the good guys. He brought my dad back to the house once when he was drunk. He had more to do with my brother, I think, and Gogs—'

Kate jumped straight in.

'He knew Casey Gogarty?'

'Gogs? Yes, he had more to do with Seth and Gogs. It was something to do with the motorcycles. It was a long time ago, Detective, you'll forgive me for not remembering every detail, I hope?'

'Of course,' Kate attempted to reassure him. 'Anything you can remember is useful.'

She made a couple of notes in her notepad.

'You know, Gogs was a great girl. If I didn't have to hide behind this damn new identity, I'd love to reach out and tell her how she helped me in my writing career. She encouraged me at a time when I was about to quit. All because of that bastard, Brewer. Anyway, Casey was a good kid, but she wasn't involved in what happened.'

'What do you know about a pact?' Charlotte asked.

'Charlotte!' Kate warned.

'I'm sorry,' she replied, 'My apologies, Josh, I'm only supposed to be an observer here. It's the journalist in me. I can't help it.'

'I think I'd like to finish now,' Josh said as he stood up and walked toward the front door. There was a knocking sound from the rear of the lodge.

'It sounds like your shower gel fell again,' Kate remarked. She gave away a small smile to Charlotte as she said it.

'As I said, Detective, these lodges creak and groan a bit. It's the wind off the bay that catches them. It's nothing to worry about.'

Josh was rushing them to the door now. He seemed suddenly anxious to see them out.

'How long will you be in the lodge, Josh, just in case we need to speak to you again?'

Kate was sounding formal again, taking care of business.

'The agreement was that I'd meet you once to see if I could help with the case. I think we're done here, it's obvious I can't be of any help—'

To their side, Charlotte and Kate became aware of the hallway door opening. It opened fully, and a man stepped out.

'I think I might be able to help you—'

It was Seth Irving, twenty-five years older than the photographs. But there was no doubt, it was Seth Irving.

FOURTEEN

'For fuck's sake, Seth! I thought we agreed—'

'It's the right thing, Josh. I can't stay hiding out the back there forever. We have to move this on.'

'I'm so bloody angry with you. This could blow everything apart. Did you ever consider that?'

'My life was blown apart already, Josh, if you remember.'

At those words, Josh lowered his head.

'Okay, I'm sorry. This is my brother, Seth, Detective. And now, I'm quite sure you're going to have a lengthy list of questions you want to ask me.'

Charlotte could tell that her face looked like she'd just won the jackpot on the fruit machines, but she didn't care; this was an incredible breakthrough.

Seth walked further into the room and sat down in the second armchair. Josh had a look of thunder all over his face.

Kate introduced herself, then explained why Charlotte was there.

'You understand that this changes things, Josh? Seth is a

person of interest in this case, and he is not subject to the same anonymity as you. This complicates matters—'

'You think I don't know that, DCI Summers? I asked Seth to keep quiet out the back. This now brings in me and my family. I'm so fucking angry with you, Seth.'

'Why are you here?' Charlotte asked. Kate didn't reprimand her. She figured things were now so fluid, it didn't matter that much if she participated.

'I'd been receiving death threats in prison, before my release. I mean, I've been receiving death threats for the past twenty-five years, that's nothing new. But these letters were something different; whoever was writing them, knew things—'

'Do you know who it was who sent them?'

'Not a clue. They were signed JI. I know it's not Josh, of course. But they're also my father's initials, if you didn't know that already—'

'Jonny Irving?' Kate confirmed.

'Yeah. But he disappeared years ago and was never seen again. You probably know that, too?'

'We do,' Kate replied. 'So how are you in contact with Josh? He's supposed to have a new identity.'

'Because I reached out to him in prison, Detective,' Josh began. He was struggling to contain his emotions and seemed to Charlotte to be wavering between anger and relief.

'Do you know what it's like knowing your brother is rotting in prison while you have your freedom back and a whole new life? It makes you feel like shit, Detective. I visited Seth several times since I was released. Nobody knew who I was. You know, I use a photograph of an actor in my books. You won't see my picture anywhere, the image on the sleeve notes is some guy I've never met before. I'm like a ghost.'

'I was scared for my life when I got out of prison,' Seth picked up. 'This person who was writing the letters knew things that only Josh and I could have known. It was stuff about our dad, our mum running away, things that happened at school. Who could have known that? Usually, the letters were from cranks or crazies. This person was going to be waiting for me when I got out. I was scared. Josh said he'd help.'

The four of them sat in silence for a few minutes, each figuring out where this revelation left them.

'Our father was not a nice man,' Josh said, finally breaking the silence. 'Seth took many punches for me when we were kids. When you see your big brother being beaten up by your dad, it's not nice, believe me. Despite my better judgement, I said he could hide out here. I smuggled him in under the cover of night. Nobody even knows he's here.'

Charlotte's brain was buzzing. She was so distracted by what was going on, she'd barely even noticed her sore ribs.

'Could it be Casey - Gogs?' she asked, 'Or, one of the other boys? Eric, or Robbie?'

'It's not Gogs,' Seth said, without any element of doubt in his voice. 'She left town and was never seen again. I've not heard from her since before the cops came round to our house to place us in custody. And, why would Eric and Robbie be responsible? There's no bad blood between us. I took the hit for all of us. If anything, they owe me. This is somebody we don't know, it's something that we've all missed.'

'What's your plan, Seth?' Kate asked. 'Now we know where you are. What do you intend on doing next?'

'Exactly!' Josh butted in as if he'd finally driven home

his point. 'What's going to happen? You're out in the open, anybody can come for you now—'

'Did you ever consider you might be at risk, too?' Charlotte asked. It had just occurred to her. 'I mean, if this person has a grudge against Seth, why not the rest of you?'

The brothers exchanged a glance. Josh spoke first.

'Well, nobody knows where Robbie and Eric are. And nobody knows where I am—'

'We have a slight problem with that,' Kate interjected, 'but I'll tell you about that before we go. I think we're going to have to find a safe place for you, Seth. Until we can work out who's got a grudge and they're safely apprehended. It seems to me that there's something we don't know about Dave Brewer's case. And, for some reason, nobody wants to share that information.'

The brothers exchanged a glance again. It was Seth who spoke first this time.

'I promise you, there is nobody else I can think of who might be doing this. I will make the letters available to you so you can search for clues. You won't find anything—'

'What makes you so sure it's not your father?' Charlotte asked. 'I mean, nobody knows where he is, do they?'

'It's not our father—'

Both men spoke at once.

'Why are you so sure?' Charlotte pushed.

'He'd be in his fifties or sixties now, Charlotte. He couldn't have done some of the things that have been done - could he?'

'He'd be sixty-one if he was still around,' Josh chimed in. 'It was only the alcohol that kept him going—'

'I'm in my mid-fifties,' Charlotte remarked. 'It doesn't mean I'm old and past it.'

'It's not our father,' Seth reiterated. 'Just take it from me. It's not Jonny.'

'So, we're no further forward, are we?' Charlotte asked. 'We have JI as initials, we know he was living in Saltburn—'

'Saltburn?' Seth asked. 'That was the postcode of these letters I received in prison—'

'He was living rough out there,' Kate added. 'We can't get a name. He's like a ghost.'

'What if he's got Casey?' Charlotte asked.

Seth was taken by surprise hearing that information.

'Casey? Gogs? Is she here, in Morecambe?'

'I'm sorry, we shouldn't have mentioned that,' Kate answered sternly, furrowing her eyebrows at her friend.

'Can I see her?' Seth asked. 'I'd love to speak to her. Do you think she'd see me?'

Kate gave Charlotte a despairing look as if she'd just let a big secret slip.

'I need to speak to her. I haven't seen her in twenty-five years. I have to explain to her. Can you arrange it, Detective?'

'Once we get you into a safe place, perhaps,' Kate began. 'I'm going to have to discuss this with my superiors, it's suddenly become complicated. But I must tell you, Seth, at this very moment, nobody knows where Casey - where Gogs – is, or if she's even safe.'

FIFTEEN

Morecambe, 1996

Adventure Kingdom was packed with locals and tourists. The air was filled with screams of delight, gasps of fear, and the chatter of happy families. This was Morecambe at its best: vibrant, fun, exciting.

Frank looked up at the mouse ride and shuddered.

'There's no way I'm going up there, Kate. Look at the height of it—'

'Coward!' Kate and Brett teased.

'You go ahead, I'll watch, and once I've seen you do it, I might join you next time.'

Kate and Brett rushed over to the queue for the next ride. Frank looked up at the top track where the metal, mouse-shaped carriage had just performed a sharp right-hand turn, making it appear as if the rider was about to be launched into oblivion. A middle-aged lady looked like she was about to leap out and take her chances with gravity. It was not for Frank, he preferred the tamer fairground rides.

'See you on the other side, chicken!' Brett shouted over as he climbed into his carriage.

Frank gave him a wave and a smile, then a thumbs-up to Kate who was next in line.

He loved family times like this. It convinced him that he was not failing with the kids. They'd chat with him, laugh and gossip, and he loved it. The only thing missing was Evie. He wished she could be there to see how well the kids were growing up; she'd be so proud of them.

With Kate now in her carriage, she shouted out, 'So long, sucker!', as her ride began. He could hear Brett laughing on the far side of the track, having a great time. This was a good evening; they all needed this.

There was a candy floss machine in one of the arcades opposite the mouse ride, so Frank walked over to surprise the kids when they finished. It never failed to amaze him how they were able to endure the ups and downs of the rides and put away ice creams, hot dogs and fizzy drinks at the same time. Their stomachs appeared to be immune to every jolt and rattle.

He looked up at the tracks to wave to Brett and Kate whenever they shot by, and he shuddered as he watched Kate's carriage traverse the sharp turn that had frightened the lady earlier. Kate had a head for heights, that was for sure. It might have been useful if he'd shared the same fear-lessness as a beat copper, but he knew his limits; heights were not his thing.

Frank paid for the candy floss and waited for the kids to re-join him. Brett came off first, high with adrenaline, gushing from the thrill of it.

'Wow, Dad, you should give it a try. It's terrifying on the corners, and some of those dips are crazy.'

Kate's carriage came to a halt, and a young fairground

assistant gave her particularly attentive service as she climbed out. His girl was growing up; she'd be a woman soon.

'Candy floss, thanks, Dad!' she exclaimed as she rushed up to them and took the treat from Frank's hand.

'I don't know how you do it,' Frank smiled at them. 'You have stronger stomachs than I ever will.'

The kids ate their candy floss and chatted between themselves as Frank took a few seconds to relish the moment. They'd lost Evie, but their family was still strong. He needed times like this to reassure himself that it would all be okay. Seeing how the kids had come to rely on each other, watching them as they laughed and chatted, he could see they'd be okay. Sure, they'd taken a big hit when their mum had died; it had knocked them for six. But sitting there in the Adventure Kingdom, the sound of the slot machines behind them, the whooshes and howls of the ghost train battling with the music from the dodgems, he saw that his family had survived.

'Okay if we go on the big dipper, Dad?' Brett asked. He'd devoured his candy floss in no time at all.

'How do you do that?' Frank asked. 'Yes, sure, here are your ride tickets. How about I meet you over by the ticket kiosk in, what, fifteen minutes?'

Kate checked her watch.

'Sure, that gives us time to go on the waltzers, too, then we can all have a final ride on the bumper cars.'

'That's more my kind of ride,' Frank smiled at Kate, kissing her on the forehead before she leapt up and ran off with Brett. He could already see glimpses of the adults they would become. He was proud of them; he and Evie had done well.

In amongst the mayhem of fairground sounds Frank

suddenly tuned into a familiar voice. It was just behind him; its tone was what struck him, but he was unable to place it out of context. He turned around to see a group of three people passing by: a woman, a man and a teenage boy. From behind, he was certain that was Jonny Irving, but he couldn't be sure.

Frank stood up and cleared away the candy floss sticks, putting them in a nearby bin. All the time, he kept his eye on the small group. It looked like a family unit, but he was certain that Jonny Irving's wife had left him. That was the word on the street at the police station.

Frank had the next ten minutes free, so he decided to tail them and get a sense of what was going on. He'd not seen Jonny like this before; he was sober and calm. Whenever Jonny Irving's name was mentioned over police radios, it was in connection with some altercation or other in a local hostelry. He didn't recognise this man's behaviour.

Frank hung back as the group stopped and walked up to the ticket kiosk. He leaned by the Test Your Strength machine, and watched..

It only took a few moments before the old Jonny was back. From a distance, it looked to Frank like he was trying to exchange some vouchers for ride tickets. There was an issue with it, and Jonny's patience was being tested. In the end, the woman who was with him dug out her purse and paid with cash.

Their first destination was the dodgems. Jonny and the woman took one car, the teenage boy took the other. It was the first time he'd got a proper look at the teenager; he was as certain as he could be that this was not one of the children that he'd seen when he and Larry returned a drunk Jonny to his house. He was a surly child, an unpleasant looking teenager. So, did Jonny have a new woman in tow?

Had he found a single parent who was happy to tolerate his bad behaviour?

Frank thought about how he'd fought to keep his own family tight after Evie's death; he wondered how much of a look-in Jonny's kids were getting. From his attitude when they'd dropped him off at the family home, Jonny Irving didn't appear to have a lot of time for Seth and the other kids.

With the bumper car ride completed, Frank hung back as Jonny and the boy made their way over to a slot ride. The coins for the ride were provided by the woman; it appeared that Jonny's pockets were empty.

Frank watched as the two of them climbed onto two full-size speedway bike simulators, each with a racing track screen positioned above the front wheel. They placed their money in the slots at the same time, high-fived each other as the screens loaded in front of them, and rode the computerised race track in perfect unison, leaning to the left, then to the right, like they were on the same team.

Watching them there together, enjoying each other's company, Frank would not have been surprised to discover that the teenage boy was Jonny's son, rather than his stepson.

SIXTEEN

'I can't believe what just happened,' Charlotte said as she climbed back into Kate's car.

She flinched as a pain shot through her chest. She moved her hand instinctively, and Kate saw it.

'Are you okay? I'm worried about you. You shouldn't be doing this, you should be in bed, resting.'

'What if I told you the same thing?' Charlotte replied. 'You've got to lie in bed while this amazing case is unravelling before your eyes. Would you take to your sickbed?'

'No, of course not. But that doesn't mean I have to stop worrying about you.'

Charlotte pulled the door shut and moved her hand over her rib cage.

'I'm certain it's the bruising that's causing the discomfort. I promise, as soon as we've run these errands, I'll see Doctor Henderson and get him to check me over. I don't have a death wish, you know, even though it might appear that way sometimes.'

Kate had already made some calls back to the office.

They'd wandered through the holiday park, looking out over the bay and towards the nuclear power station.

It had been decided that Seth and Josh might just as well stay in the holiday lodge; they were as secure there as anywhere. The caravan site was packed with holiday-makers, so they were as anonymous as they could be. Seth was the main concern. Josh could pretty well come and go as he pleased. Kate had noticed that a static caravan opposite Josh's lodge was empty and for sale.

'We'll get a couple of officers stationed in there to keep an eye on them. If they stay in plain clothes and keep their heads down, we can maintain a 24-hour watch on them. If Seth stays out of sight, it'll be fine until this all blows over.'

By the time Kate started the car to head off to the industrial estate, the situation was as managed as it could be.

'Right, Baker's Breakers, then home for you,' Kate said as she put the car in reverse and backed out of the parking space.

Charlotte was constantly amazed at the variety of businesses that were located on White Lund Industrial Estate. She'd never seen Baker's Breakers before, even though she'd driven through the estate many times. It was tucked at the end of a cul-de-sac on a road she'd never had cause to drive down. Kate drove the car through the gap in the spiked, iron fence and parked it up in front of a world-weary caravan which served as the office. The scrapyard seemed vast to Charlotte; she hadn't a clue how the industrial estate managed to accommodate a business of that size. The mangled cars were neatly stacked four high. There was a forklift truck pulled up outside the caravan and a huge crane, which operated a giant grasp, parked in the centre of the yard. Charlotte watched from the car as a wreck of a car was moved from one side of the yard to the other, as if the crane was a movie Transformer annihilating its foe.

'I've never been in one of these places before,' Charlotte remarked. 'It's not a place to visit in your high heels.'

There were oily puddles of water around the yard, which was lined with stacked up starter motors and stripped-out car parts. There were oil cans jam-packed with wiper blades, starter motors, car batteries and all sorts of salvaged vehicle parts. To their right was a row of motorcycles, in various states of repair. Some looked like they were ready to ride off, others had been picked clean as if vultures had torn the flesh off a carcass.

'Okay, let's see if Mr Baker is in,' Kate said, opening her door. 'If you need to rest, feel free to sit this one out. It won't take long.'

Charlotte opened her door and stepped out. A spasm ran through her chest once again, and, for one moment, she wondered if she'd pushed herself too far, too soon. The pain subsided, so she closed the door and joined Kate as she headed for the caravan. The words *Site Office* were spray-painted on the side. The caravan looked like it belonged on top of one of the scrap piles; it had seen better days. Its once-white exterior was now dulled by lichen, its windows were steamed up and spattered with dried mud.

Kate put a foot on the small step that had been placed outside, and peered inside the door.

'Hello, DCI Kate Summers,' she said.

They were expected.

'Ah, DCI Summers, come in, come in. Thanks for driving out here.'

Charlotte followed Kate into the caravan which shook as it took their weight. The interior had been stripped out so that only the sink and the window seat area remained.

Charlotte clocked the nudes calendar on the wall to the side of a battered filing cabinet. Her instinct was to comment, but she decided to save it for later. A man was working at a desk strewn with paperwork. He was wearing oily overalls, and his hands were so caked in grease, it seemed like he might have been born that way. He had a black, bushy beard streaked with grey.

Kate made the introductions. There were two seats available to them on their side of the desk, but they looked like they'd weathered a thousand storms. The upholstery was worn and threadbare and appeared to be impregnated with a thin layer of oil.

'I'm Bobby Baker,' the man said, standing up. 'I'll take you outside to the bikes; it's a bit of a mess in here.'

As Bobby led the way, Charlotte nodded at the calendar of nudes on the wall.

'Good job it's not November yet, Bobby might have recognised me from his calendar.'

Kate stifled a laugh. Charlotte straightened her face as Bobby turned to speak to them.

'Although this place looks like a bomb hit it, we do have a system. We have to keep records of the vehicles; the days of disposing of dodgy cars are long gone.'

He walked them over to the motorcycles.

'We take all types of scrap here, not just cars. We have bikes, vans and even elite scrap vehicles over the back there. There are washing machines too, behind the caravan. I even have a couple of caravans right over the far end. You'd be surprised what folks scavenge.'

'When did you realise the motorcycle was missing?' Kate asked.

'Yesterday,' Bobby replied, searching in the pockets of his overalls. He drew out a folded piece of paper and handed it to Kate. She opened it up and passed it to Charlotte.

The paper was warm where it had been stewing in Bobby's pocket. Charlotte tried to remove the image from her mind. There were oily fingerprints on the paper where he'd handled it. She examined the paper. There was a picture of a motorcycle printed on it, with some basic information about the vehicle below. Bobby's printer had probably seen better days as the printing was streaked and erratic.

A bell sounded across the yard. Charlotte and Kate looked at Bobby, both wondering what it was.

'It's just the phone,' he explained, 'I have it piped through the yard so I can hear it when I'm out of the office.'

With that explained, Charlotte studied the printout again. Bobby seemed in no hurry to answer the phone.

'That's the bike,' she confirmed.

'You're sure?' Kate asked.

'Definitely.'

'Whoever took it stole a number plate off that pile over there,' Bobby added. 'I can't tell you what it is before you ask me. But the chassis number is on that piece of paper, so that might help.'

'How did he get in?' Charlotte asked. 'That fencing looks pretty secure around this compound. Did he just walk in and take it?'

'There's only two of us on this site,' Bobby answered. 'If I get caught up with a customer on the site, people can walk in and out of here. I mean, it's not as if the cars are in working order, is it?'

'So how did he manage to ride off on a motorcycle that was destined for scrap?' Kate pushed.

'Well, there's the thing, you see. There wasn't much

wrong with that bike, it was a runner, it just needed a bit of work. Whoever took it must have known about bikes. To wander in here like that, fix the spark plugs in a matter of minutes and hotwire it without the key, he must have worked with motorcycles before.'

SEVENTEEN

Nigel sat at his desk with his mouth wide open.

'I don't know what to say,' he began, shaking his head. 'You shouldn't even be alive, Charlotte. Please don't mention this to Teddy. If he knows how much jeopardy his staff indemnity insurance is in, he'll have a cardiac arrest—'

'That'll be two of us then,' Charlotte smiled.

'Don't joke about it,' Nigel frowned. 'It doesn't bear thinking about. I take it Will is delighted with you?'

'Don't mention Will. I think he's in a state of despair. But you know what it's like, Nigel. You get a great news story, you can't let it rest. Personally, I think you're a slacker. If you haven't been threatened with torture, almost pushed out the back of a wind turbine or electrocuted at a fairground, I think we have to question your dedication to the profession.'

Nigel laughed.

'If you can do your best to stay alive long enough, I booked First Class tickets to London from Morecambe for the awards ceremony. Teddy's pushing out the boat. He has high hopes.'

'I hope he's not too let down when I don't win it. I haven't even finished off my correspondence course yet. They can't give an award to an apprentice when the grand-masters are around. I'm just treating it as a good night out. You got my email with my guest list?'

'Yes, and Teddy okayed it. You really are the golden girl at the moment. Please don't screw it up by getting into any more trouble.'

Charlotte wished she could tell Nigel the full story, but Kate had sworn her to secrecy. Josh and Seth's presence in the resort had to remain top secret; she understood that. She also hung back on Casey's disappearance. She'd endured a long lecture from Kate on the drive back from the industrial estate, reminding her about the things that might prejudice the case or place the lives of key players at risk.

'Okay, I'm walking over to the library, then I'm going to get some bed rest,' Charlotte announced. 'If there's anything more to report, I'll let you know.'

Charlotte was disappointed to see that Reagan wasn't on the reception desk when she left the newspaper office. The stand-in informed her that she was attending her college course. Charlotte had hoped they might arrange the evening out in town that they'd discussed.

She was deep in thought as she walked over to the library. She was churning over everything they now knew. Whatever scraps of information they'd managed to gather, it all boiled down to a couple of things. They needed to speak to Casey, and they had to find out who JI was. She thought about the man who'd chased her. She'd seen his face before he dropped the electrical cable in the puddle. Everything about him suggested he wasn't in his fifties or sixties; it was a younger man. So, it couldn't have been Jonny Irving.

Jon Rogers had made himself scarce in the library, and it

took two members of staff to track him down. That was more like the Jon she knew. He took her into his office. It looked like a school classroom in the final week of term; he was starting to strip the walls and clear out of there. Retirement was almost upon him.

'Hi, Charlotte, thanks for coming over. I've got a surprise for you.'

'Did you receive the press cuttings and photographs that were sent over from the newspaper archive?' she asked.

'I did, thank you so much for doing that. It turns out we do have the archive material; it had been removed from the building. We don't allow that, but whoever came to look at it walked out with it and didn't return it.'

'How did you get it back?' Charlotte asked.

'Some kind soul found it dumped at the roadside in a plastic supermarket bag. All the documents have the library stamp on them, so they found their way back to us eventually.'

'That's good news at least. Now, you have a brilliant archive, what with the new information Nigel sent over from the newspaper.'

Charlotte wasn't sure why Jon had called her over. She was feeling tired out now and was ready to have a sit-down. Maybe Will and Kate were right; she did need to take it easy.

'Well, it's not all good news,' Jon continued. 'Whoever took these materials hasn't taken a lot of care. For starters, not everything has been returned. Some photos have been cut out of the old newspapers, and there are a lot of underlined names and locations, too, all in pen, of course, so they can't be erased.'

'So, do you know who took them?' Charlotte asked. She was anxious to get home now.

'Yes, that's why I called you over,' Jon smiled. 'You're not the only sleuth around here. I found an item of personal documentation in the pile of papers. Whoever was using this archive got careless—'

He picked up a cardboard wallet from his desk and drew out a series of passport photographs. There should have been four images, but one of them had been cut out. Charlotte recognised the person immediately; it was the man who'd tried to kill her.

She took photos on her phone and texted them to Kate. *This is our man! Will explain later.*

'Was there anything else in there?' Charlotte asked.

'No, but wait a moment, I haven't told you everything yet,' Jon continued. 'I know this man. Well, I knew him, at least. He used to be local—'

'Do you know his name?' Charlotte asked, finally grasping where Jon was heading with this.

'I do. In fact, I can do much better than that. This man has his own place in the archive.'

Jon placed his hand in the cardboard wallet and drew out two photocopies of newspaper articles.

'I printed these off from the microfiche, I assumed you'd want to take some copies away with you.'

Charlotte scanned the headlines.

Morecambe Arsonist Behind Bars.

Morecambe Youth Obsessed With Fire. Compulsion, Judge Says.

'Damn, this is the man we're trying to find,' Charlotte said to herself as much as to Jon. 'He has past form. No wonder everything's about fire, look at this news story—'

She scanned the details of the news reports. Rory Higson's name was in the byline. It was dated 1999.

A youth who left a trail of destruction in Morecambe has

been sentenced to two years in custody after a lengthy police investigation succeeded in catching him in the act.

'This is amazing, Jon. Talk about a great discovery. I'm just trying to find his name in here.'

'It's not in there,' Jon replied. 'He was too young to be named in the newspaper. But, I know him. The paper might not be able to print his name, but Morecambe is a small resort. Everybody knows everybody. You know how it is.'

Charlotte could barely contain her excitement. At least her heart was functioning properly; she could feel it pounding in her chest.

'So, what do the initials JI stand for?' she asked. 'I can't believe you've been able to help with this—'

'JI?' Jon queried. 'I can help you with half of that. His name is Jimmy Rylands. A right little terror, he was. I don't know where the initial 'I' came from.'

EIGHTEEN

Morecambe, 1996

'You go and check on the old lady, and I'll take a walk over to Heysham Moss. That way we can kill two birds with one stone, and catch a decent lunch break.'

Larry didn't take much convincing. Frank knew the mention of a long lunch break would catch his attention. They'd been heading out to run a second check on Heysham Moss when the call had come in on the radio. An old lady had taken a fall in a nearby property; Frank and Larry picked it up as they were in the area.

'Besides, there's not likely to be any activity on the Moss since we picked up that motorcycle. They'll have all made themselves scarce by now.'

Larry nodded in agreement, and they headed their separate ways. Frank had the longer walk, but he was happy for it; the weather was decent, and it was a good day to be out on foot.

The moment he turned down Meldon Road and neared the railway crossing he heard the roar of a motorcycle. He stopped and listened for a moment, trying to figure out which direction it had come from. There were two bikes out there; he'd catch them in the act. This was good for the police campaign; so far it had yielded poor results.

Heysham Moss was a mixture of grassland, wooded areas, moss land and bracken. It was the perfect place to walk the dog or take the kids on an adventure. It also made an excellent location for teenage bikers to take their vehicles out for a spin.

Frank made his way over to a wooded spot that seemed to be home to the closest engine sound. As he pushed through the long grass, he spotted a figure perched on a motorbike, motionless behind a bush. The engine was idling, but the rider appeared to be hiding.

Whoever was concealed behind the helmet, they hadn't yet spotted Frank. They were alert to something else.

'Hey!' Frank shouted.

The motorcycle rider switched off their engine.

That was the last thing Frank had expected. He'd been prepared for a fast getaway and having to scribble down the number plate. The rider's hands moved to their helmet and lifted it off their head. Frank got his second surprise. He'd expected a young man, but underneath the helmet was a young woman wearing the thickest glasses Frank had ever seen.

'Oh, thank God you're here,' the girl said. 'Someone is chasing me through these woods—'

Frank saw the look of panic in her eyes. He didn't know this girl, but she seemed well-spoken, not the sort of person he'd expect to find out churning up the Moss.

'Woa, steady, take a breath, and tell me what's going on. I'm PC Allan, Frank Allan. What's your name first of all?'

'I'm Casey. Casey Gogarty—'

'Do you have a licence to drive this bike, Casey?'

'I do, yes. I'm seventeen. I don't have it on me. The bike is 125cc, so I'm fine to ride it on the road—'

'But this isn't the road, is it, Casey?'

Frank checked himself. He was giving this poor girl a hard time when she'd already told him she was scared. This was not the time to give her a dressing down.

'I'm sorry, Casey, I was being overzealous. We've had a lot of trouble with teenage riders on this patch. Tell me what the problem is.'

He looked at the girl as she spoke. It was a wonder she could see to ride with those glasses. He reckoned she must be around Kate's age. He wondered if they knew each other.

'You don't know Kate Allan, do you? Are you still at the school? She must be in your year group.'

'No,' Casey answered, 'I don't know her. I've probably seen her around. She must be the year above, or below, mine. I'd know her if she was in my year, I think.'

'It was just a thought. Now, tell me what's bothering you.'

The sound of a thrashed motorcycle engine came from the other side of the trees. A look of fear washed over Casey's face.

'There's a man been chasing me on a motorbike—'

'What do you mean by chasing?'

'He followed me over from Morecambe. I came out for a ride. I didn't realise he was behind me until I got here.'

Frank resisted the urge to remind her that she shouldn't be riding out on the Moss.

'Is that him I can hear now?'

'Yes. He's stalking me. He's been trying to intimidate me. I'm scared to death. I thought he was going to hurt me out here.'

'And, that's why you're hiding behind this bush?'

'Yes. I was waiting until he got fed up and went away.'

'Look, Casey, I'm going to ask you to push your bike back to the road, then go home. I want you to promise me you won't come out here again—'

'I just come to practise my motocross. It's a great place to do it—'

'I'm sure it is, Casey, but it's illegal to ride here. I should be booking you right now, but I can see how frightened you are. You push your bike off that way, over the railway crossing, and I'll find your man and see what he's playing at. Deal?'

'Okay,' Casey replied. 'Thank you.'

She placed the helmet back on her head, climbed off the bike, and pushed it in the direction of the railway. Frank watched her a while, then emerged from the foliage and found the footpath once again. He could hear the second bike not far away now, it was running at a low speed like the rider was trying to flush someone out of hiding.

Frank circled the trees, looking back at regular intervals to check that Casey had made her exit. He could see she was clear now; she'd be back on the road and on her way to Morecambe already.

He saw the rider up ahead and waved over to him. The rider stopped a moment, lifted his visor and stared at him. It was too far away for Frank to see the face, but everything about the rider's stance and build suggested it was a man.

'Can I have a word?' Frank shouted over, walking through the long grass to close the distance between them.

The rider gave him the finger, pulled down his visor, then heavily revved the bike. It blew out a fog of exhaust fumes. The rider pulled a wheelie, then started to move at speed towards him. Frank began to dodge, seeing that he was now a target, and he called at the motorcyclist to stop.

The bike was coming directly for him, at some speed. Frank stood still, waiting and watching the rider, trying to second guess which way he should dive for cover. At the last possible moment, he leapt to the left as the front wheel was just in front of his right knee. He gambled correctly as the bike veered to the right, the rider's elbow clipping Frank's as he crashed to the ground.

The rider revved the engine once more, pulled out of a skid and raced off toward the exit to the Moss. As Frank crashed to the floor, he turned his head in a desperate attempt to catch the number plate. He didn't need a registration number to identify the bike. It was the same motorcycle he'd seen Seth Irving riding at Whinnysty Lane only two weeks previously.

NINETEEN

Charlotte felt the energy drain from her body. She'd already done too much, she knew that, but the dead-end of the surname Rylands made her feel like everything they did wound up in a cul-de-sac.

'You're certain of that?' she checked with Jon.

'Definitely. Rylands was the name. He was a kid from a broken home, you know the story. His mum had a procession of unsuitable men in her life. The kid couldn't stop setting things on fire.'

'Is the mother still around?'

'That I don't know, Charlotte. You'll have to ask your pals at the police station. I'm sure they can find that out faster than I can.'

'Do you have a phone directory around?' Charlotte asked.

'What's one of those?' Jon laughed. 'Actually, and no teasing, please, I do have one. It's old and tatty, but it still works. You don't even have to reboot it before you look up a phone number. It's over here in my bottom drawer—'

Jon walked over to his desk, opened up the drawer and

pulled out a dog-eared Morecambe phone directory, holding it up like an Olympian might show off a medal.

'They're useful to have around,' Jon smiled. 'Even looking up a simple phone number is a hassle these days.'

Charlotte took the directory off him and navigated to the surname Rylands.

'There aren't that many Rylands in the resort. What year is this?'

She flipped over the directory to check the year.

'This is 2005, Jon. That's ancient. Why have you hung on to this all this time?'

'I'm the archivist, of course,' Jon replied. 'Besides, it's handy. It has addresses in it. I'm amazed they ever got away with it from a privacy point of view. Talk about a system that's wide open to abuse.'

Charlotte flipped the directory open once again.

'Any idea where she lived?'

'The newspaper article mentions the West End of Morecambe. Did you spot that Rylands torched the house that your teacher was murdered in?'

'What?' Charlotte asked.

'Yes, didn't you clock that?'

'I only skimmed the articles—'

'He burned down the house that David Brewer was murdered in. It was his first big fire. After that, there was no stopping him. He went on a burning spree until the police finally caught him.'

'This must be our man. I've heard a suggestion of a fifth child. Could that be him, I wonder?'

Jon gave her a blank look.

'I'm no police officer,' he began, 'and I can't help with that. How are you doing with that phone book?'

'Sefton Road, that's West End, isn't it? I tell you what,

I'll take a photo of the Rylands entries, and then I can pass it on to Kate.'

Charlotte took a couple of photos to make sure at least one of them was sharp enough, then texted one directly to Kate.

Our man is Jimmy Rylands. Lived in West End. Was an arsonist. Can't explain initials. Can you check if his mum is still in the resort?

She'd received a text from Kate about the passport photos she'd sent over earlier.

Call me asap. If you're sure, we can release it to the press.

Before leaving, Charlotte took photos of the newspaper articles and sent them over to Kate. She paused a moment, and considered sending them to Nigel. It felt like an act of journalistic betrayal. The identity of this mystery killer was not in the public arena yet. She'd send them over the moment the police made it public they were looking for him. That wouldn't be too long now Jon had discovered the passport photos.

Charlotte thanked Jon and caught a taxi back to the guest house. She was exhausted already and frustrated that her body could barely yet sustain a couple of routine visits.

She crept in the back door, hoping that Will and Lucia had made a lazy start to their day. It was past 11 o'clock, but both Lucia and Will had been known to lounge around in their beds that late over the summer break. She hoped it was one of those days.

The kitchen was quiet, the tables set up for evening meals, and Isla and whoever was assisting her that morning would have left the premises well over an hour ago.

She began to walk up the stairs to the family accommodation. On the second floor, she stopped by Casey's room. The door was closed, as she'd left it. For a moment she considered tapping at the door. Would that alert Will and Lucia? She decided against it.

Instead, she continued up to the family accommodation, negotiating the squeaking door and making it unnoticed to the bedroom. She placed her hand gently on the handle and pushed it down as quietly as she could. For a moment she thought she'd made it. But as the bedroom door swung open, Will and Doctor Henderson were waiting for her, the bedsheets thrown off, and her pathetic attempt at shaping a human body out of clothing exposed.

'There you are!' Will exclaimed. 'What the hell have you been up to?'

'I did warn you that you need to take things carefully, Charlotte,' the doctor added.

For a moment, she considered lying. But Henderson was right, she was overcome by fatigue already, even half a morning of light activity had taken it out of her.

'I'm sorry, hands up. I got a lift up to the library to see Jon, the archivist there. I took a taxi back. I've been taking it easy, I promise. Oh, and I popped into the office while I was in town—'

Charlotte figured the visit to Josh was confidential, so she was justified in not mentioning that.

'I thought we agreed you'd stop this,' Will began.

'It's okay,' Henderson interrupted, holding up his hand. 'Let me run some checks on your wife; it looks like there's no harm done here.'

Will looked at Charlotte, and for a moment, she thought he was going to have a go at her. Instead, he shrugged and walked to the door.

'Okay,' he said, 'but I'm going to put padlocks on this room if I have to. You must rest, Charlotte.'

Charlotte and Henderson waited for him to leave.

'I'm grateful for the time I had with your husband,' Henderson began, 'I think we've put our previous troubles behind us now. He actually thanked me for saving your life; can you believe that?'

'Not really,' Charlotte said.

Henderson left the room for a couple of minutes while Charlotte changed back into clothing that was better suited for sitting in bed. When he returned, he re-attached her to the electronic monitor, ran some tests and checked her ribs.

'You'll be feeling some chest discomfort now you're moving about?' he asked.

'You can say that again. Is it anything to worry about?'

'No, it's bruising from the chest compressions. The defibrillator won't have helped, either. Your heart is fine, it's strong, you're going to be okay. But, your body has experienced a massive shock. I don't want to sound like your dad, but you do need to be careful, Charlotte. I just want to be certain we're out of the woods.'

'Well, I'm ready to take to my bed now,' Charlotte reassured him, 'I can't believe how wiped out I feel—'

There was a knock at the door. It was Lucia.

'Hi, Mum. Isla asked me to pass this note on to you when I saw you. She found it tucked in the bookings diary when she came in this morning. She said it might have been there for a day or two and apologised for not spotting it sooner.'

'Thanks, Lucia,' Charlotte replied. 'Come over here, sit by the bed. I want to chat once Doctor Henderson is finished here.'

Lucia took a chair by the bed, and Charlotte opened the note. It was from Casey.

Charlotte. Just in case, I thought I'd better leave you a note. I'm meeting a contact in Morecambe this evening. It could be amazing for the documentary. I'm a bit concerned about him, so I'm meeting him in public. Anyway, just in case, this is his mobile number. See you soon. Casey.

A mobile telephone number was scribbled at the bottom of the paper. If Kate's team hadn't extracted the number from Casey's mobile phone already, they'd now got this confirmation of a direct line to the killer. Finally, they might be able to reach him and discover where Casey had got to.

TWENTY

Charlotte passed on the mobile phone number to Kate. She craved rest; she had to pass it on for somebody else to deal with. Henderson topped up her drugs supply after altering her doses. She caught up with Lucia, then checked her phone for messages before rolling over to shut her eyes. Kate had texted.

6.30 pm press conference at the Winter Gardens. We're issuing the passport photo to the press, but we can't name him yet. It'll be on TV. I DON'T expect to see you there!!!

There was also a message from Nigel.

They're holding a press conference at 6.30. Can you tell me anything?

Charlotte was too tired to send a reply. She made sure the phone was on charge, then rolled over and shut her eyes. Giving in to the tiredness was glorious. She offered no resistance and felt herself drifting off straight away.

She awoke with a start.

'I thought you might want to see this.'

It was Will. He was holding a laptop on which something was streaming.

'What time is it?' Charlotte asked.

'Just after half-past six. You've been crashed out for hours. You must have needed the rest.'

Charlotte sat up in bed. Will kicked off his slippers and sat up beside her, the laptop perched on his knees.

'This is the press conference, isn't it?' Charlotte asked.

'I figured this was the best compromise,' Will began. 'If you can't attend the press conference, let the press conference come to you.'

'Wow, they're leading the regional news programme with it,' Charlotte observed. 'It's hit the big time now.'

The news show was taking a live feed of the press conference. The cameras were trained on a table on which three microphones had been set up. The backdrop was the stage at the Winter Gardens. Suddenly, cameras started flashing, and Toni Lawson, Detective Superintendent Amanda Pickering and Kate walked out and took their positions at the table.

Toni began speaking first.

'Thank you for joining us for the press conference this evening—'

The TV camera made a sweep across the room of assembled journalists and reporters. She spotted Nigel sitting there with his shorthand pad, and Milo had made a second appearance, too. She felt her hackles rising but calmed herself. They'd made a truce, they were friends now, however testing that might be for her.

Toni continued with her update. Charlotte leaned over to check her phone.

'As members of the press will know, we are searching for a man who has killed two people and made attempts to kill several others. In most cases, he has used arson to threaten the lives of the individuals involved. So far, we have been unable to identify this man. But, we are now in a position to share this photograph of a man who we wish to question in connection with our investigation—'

Even though it was Charlotte who'd sent over the image, she still couldn't resist shouting out when she saw it on the TV.

'That's the picture I sent to Kate. They're using it on the television.'

Will smiled and kissed her.

'It's your TV debut,' he teased, 'The offers of work will come flooding in now.'

Toni continued.

'Members of the public are asked not to approach this man if they see him, but to call the incident room number, instead.'

Toni read out the number twice, then handed it over to DSU Amanda Pickering. It looked like the Assistant Chief Constable had chickened out this time around, after the last press conference had descended into a rabble at the hands of Milo De Vries.

'I would like to reassure the public that we are putting as many resources as we can spare onto this case. I would also like to reiterate that people should remain calm and circumspect, while this investigation is ongoing. Several elements of the press have tried to connect this case with the murder of the teacher David Brewer twenty-five years ago. At the moment, that connection is not confirmed—'

'Like fuck it isn't!' Charlotte blurted out.

'Language, Charlotte, please,' Will mock-scolded her. 'Remember, the police have to pace the release of information. You of all people should know that.'

'I do,' Charlotte replied, 'But surely the link with Brewer's case is obvious to everybody now.'

DSU Pickering handed over to Kate, who shared some more details of the investigation, then opened up to questions.

'This should be fun,' Charlotte said. 'What's the bet Milo drops another bomb?'

'I'm warming to that kid,' Will replied. 'He makes Lucia laugh her head off. He was so level-headed when you picked a fight with that electrical cable at the fairground—'

Charlotte gently dug him in the ribs.

'Don't do the same to me,' she warned, 'I'm sore at the moment.'

She looked down at her phone while the roving microphone was being taken to the first journalist for their question. Kate had texted.

I'm coming round after the press conference. I have a special request. I need to make it personally. PS Happy to give you an autograph after my TV appearance :-)

'Is the death of local funeral director Edwin Franklin connected with the case?' a BBC TV reporter asked.

Kate picked up the answer. They were just getting warmed up, Charlotte knew that much by now.

'How do you defend the leaking of information about one of the children whose identities are protected by law?'

Charlotte didn't recognise the reporter this time. DSU Pickering picked it up for a reply.

'I would like to stress that although a social media posting error was made, it was quickly deleted, and the identity and location of the person were never made public. The Police and Crime Commissioner has issued a public apology for the error through her office, and we now consider the matter closed. I would add, however, that in a case of this gravity, we'll leave no stone unturned in our hunt for the killer.'

'Good answer,' Will chipped in. 'Very diplomatic.'

'Here it comes,' Charlotte said excitedly, as the roving microphone made its way to Milo De Vries. 'You've got to admire the kid; he works hard and he doesn't let go.'

'Hi, I'm Milo De Vries from InternetRevelations.tube—'

'Get that self-promotion in Milo, well done,' Charlotte laughed.

'What's your question, Mr De Vries?' Kate asked. Charlotte could imagine her hackles rising. She did a great job of keeping a straight face.

'I don't have a question as such. I just wanted to let everybody know that I'll be revealing something about this case that everybody has missed at 9 am on my InternetRevelations.tube website tomorrow morning—'

'Thank you Mr De Vries, but this is a press conference, not a programme schedule,' DSU Pickering interrupted. The TV camera panned to Milo as a member of Toni's press team attempted to wrestle the microphone away from him.

'That's 9 o'clock on InternetRevelations.tube. I'll be exposing a secret that nobody else has told you. Believe me, you won't want to miss it.'

TWENTY-ONE

Morecambe, 1996

'You've been quiet since we left Heysham,' Larry remarked. 'Don't tell me you're so stunned by the natural beauty of the Moss that you're lost for words?'

'Not quite,' Frank laughed, shaken out of his thoughts. 'Remember that young lad on the motorcycle at Whinnysty Lane the other day? I just saw that bike again. Only whoever was riding it was bothering some young girl. She can't have been more than Kate's age. That's not right, is it?'

'Well, you said it was Jonny Irving's lad, didn't you? Why don't we drive around there now? At the very least, we can put the frighteners on him, so he doesn't do it again.'

'Yes, you're right. That young lady was terrified. We can't have guys going around doing things like that. Let's head there now before we get a call on the radio. There's no time like the present.'

Larry knew the way, and they were at the estate within five minutes.

'Let's park along the road, Larry. I don't want to alert

the entire neighbourhood. Gently does it on this one. The younger kids might be at home.'

Larry pulled up well away from the house, and the two officers climbed out of the car. As they walked up the drive, there was the smell of petrol fumes wafting through the air.

'Looks like whoever it was is home,' Larry remarked, grimacing at the odour.

'One moment,' Frank said, as Larry was about to knock on the door. He tried the side door of the garage. It was locked. He put his ear to the door.

'I can hear the metal clicking where the engine had been hot,' he called over to Larry. Frank walked around the back, to see if there was a window. There was, but it was covered in lichen. He scraped an area with his thumbnail and peered through the small area he'd cleared. It was too dark in there to see anything. Finally, he walked around the front and tugged at the garage door. Not only did it fail to open, it felt to Frank like it might be rusted shut.

'Okay, give them a knock,' he said as he re-joined Larry at the door. 'Gently does it though, let's not frighten them off.'

Larry gave a tap. There was movement inside the house. The door opened. A younger child answered, a plastic pen in his hand.

'Dad's not in,' he said before Frank and Larry had introduced themselves.

'I'm PC Frank Allan and this is my colleague, PC Larry Schofield. What's your name?'

'Josh. Josh Irving.'

'Has your dad been around today, Josh?' Larry asked.

'He comes and goes as he pleases. He was just here—'

'On the motorcycle?' Frank interrupted.

'Yeah. Seth's motorcycle. It's not his. He took it from Seth.'

Frank gave Larry a look.

'Where's your brother today? Is he around?'

'He's gone out. I don't know where. He stormed off when my dad took the bike out. He was pretty angry.'

'Do you know a young girl who wears glasses?' Frank asked. He was reluctant to draw attention to the thickness of the frames. He'd been at school once, he knew how kids became defined by these things.

'Big, thick ones? Yeah, that's Gogs. Or, Goggles—'

'Do you know her real name, son? And where she lives?'

Frank could see they were drawing a blank here. It was time to move on. At least they'd ascertained that it was Jonny on the bike.

'It's Casey, I think. She's my brother's mate really, she's not in the same year as me. We just call her by her nickname. Gogarty, that's her last name. Is she in trouble?'

'No, no,' Frank did his best to reassure him. 'Not at all, we'd just like to pop over to her house and have a word with her.'

Josh seemed uncertain, and Frank didn't want to scare him off.

'Is everything alright here, Josh? You know, if there's anything you need to tell us, we're always here to help.'

Josh looked toward the garage, then down to his feet. For a moment, it seemed like he was about to say something, but he stalled and clammed up again.

'Everything's just great here, PC Allan; it's like one big party.'

'Okay,' Frank said. 'If you ever need to speak to me, you can reach me on this number - can I borrow your pen?'

Josh handed it over, and Frank scribbled his number on a scrap of paper he found in his pocket.

Josh took the paper and placed it in his pocket. He closed the door.

'That's never seeing the light of day again,' Larry remarked as they headed down the driveway.

'I'm worried about those kids,' Frank said, deep in thought. 'Imagine being stuck with a father like Jonny Irving. It would be like a prison; you couldn't escape as a child. What are their options? Stay in that house, or get taken into care. I don't fancy either of them.'

'Should you have given him your home number though, Frank? I'm not sure that was a wise thing to do.'

Larry was displaying uncharacteristic diligence. Frank wasn't used to this level of scrutiny from his work colleague.

'If that was your child, wouldn't you want someone looking out for them?' he asked.

'Yes, but there's a procedure—'

'I know there's a procedure, Larry, but there's no way that young lad is calling the station if he gets into trouble. Call it good old-fashioned policing. It's what the village bobby would have done in my youth. If that was one of my kids, I'd like to think somebody would do the same for them.'

Frank could see that Larry wasn't convinced. He didn't have kids, how could he know? He dropped the subject.

'How about we check in on this Gogs before we head back to base? I'd just like to make sure she's okay.'

Larry nodded. They'd got the address confirmed by Control; it was on the estate and was easier to walk over to rather than moving the car. Within five minutes, they were standing by the drive.

Frank surveyed the house and garden before moving on.

'Amazing how some people keep their houses so nicely on this estate, and the Jonny Irvings of the world don't give a damn. You'd think he'd want to live in a nice place, wouldn't you?'

They walked up the short driveway and knocked on the door. There was no car parked outside, but that wasn't unusual on the estate; most of the residents didn't run cars. Pop music could be heard from a room upstairs. Larry knocked again, much more forcefully this time. The music stopped, and they heard the thud of footsteps down the staircase. The door opened. The girl with the thick glasses opened the door. The contrast between this house and the Irving's couldn't have been starker. It was nicely decorated, tidy and homely. There was laminate in the hallway.

Frank stepped forward so she'd recognise him.

'Hi, Casey, it's PC Allan again, we just chatted over at Heysham Moss—'

'Oh, hi PC Allan. My mum and dad are shopping in Lancaster; they're not in—'

'Well, it's you I wanted to check on, Casey. This is my colleague, PC Schofield by the way. Are you okay? You were very shaken when I last saw you.'

Casey seemed like she was about to speak, then halted.

'Is everything alright?' Frank asked gently.

'I don't want my mum and dad to know,' she began. 'They've asked me not to ride on dirt tracks—'

'Well, I told you the same thing, Casey. But let's forget that for now. There's no need for me to tell your parents about that if you promise me, you won't do it again.'

'Okay,' Casey nodded.

'So, is there anything you want to tell me?' Frank suggested.

'That man on the motorcycle. It was Mr Irving. I know

two of his kids, they're friends of mine. They're nothing like him—'

'Go on,' Larry encouraged her.

'Mr Irving took Seth's motorbike and locked it up in his garage. He keeps hassling me now, ever since I went round to help Josh with his writing. He keeps asking questions about my dad's work. And, he makes horrible suggestions to me about—'

She stalled. She was struggling to find the words.

'It's okay, Casey. You can tell us,' Frank said.

'He talks about private stuff. I'm only seventeen. He shouldn't be saying things like that, should he? I was scared when he followed me to Heysham Moss today. I want him to stop.'

TWENTY-TWO

'If Nigel tried that with The Bay View Weekly, we'd shift more copies, that's for sure.'

Charlotte was in awe of Milo's overconfident self-promotion. For the second time, he'd created a huge stir at a bland press conference.

'You have to admire him,' Will agreed. 'That's how you make sure the world is tuned in. I'll be watching now, won't you?'

'Steady, Will, before you know it, you'll be caught up in the story and running around chasing bad guys. Even worse, you might become a Milonite.'

Charlotte meant it as a tease, but it was also a small dig at Will. He was as hooked as she was at developments in the murder case. Only, she had a direct line of access, and it was difficult to back off.

Charlotte's phone buzzed. It was Kate.

FFS. Did you see that kid? OK to come round? Need to chat.

'Kate's on her way,' Charlotte ventured. Will said

nothing so she assumed it was safe to go on. 'She only wants a quick chat.'

'Best make sure Milo is scarce when she comes,' Will laughed. 'I don't want a brawl breaking out in the dining room.'

He swung his legs off the bed and closed the lid on the laptop. The news had reverted to talented pet stories and parochial fillers.

'I'll get some food on,' Will offered. 'Are you alright to join us?'

'Yes, I'll pull some clothes on,' Charlotte replied. 'I feel a hell of a lot better after that sleep.'

Fifteen minutes later, Will and Charlotte were eating at the table, and Kate's voice travelled up the stairs from the ground floor. Shortly afterwards, there was a knock at the door which separated the family quarters from the upper landing.

'Hi, Kate,' Charlotte smiled as she opened the door to greet her friend, who looked washed out and fed up. 'Bad day?'

'You could say that,' Kate replied. 'There's a lot of shit and red tape in this job, you know. You're looking a lot better than when I last saw you. You looked knackered when I dropped you off at the library.'

'Can I get you a fish finger sandwich, Kate?' Will asked. 'You must be famished after that press conference. We have some spare.'

'You weren't watching, were you?' Kate asked, scrunching up her face into a cringe.

'Sorry, we were,' Will answered. 'You did well, it was good.'

'I'd rather put it behind me,' Kate continued. 'Yes, I will have that fish finger sandwich, thank you.'

She sat opposite Charlotte at the table as Will took the leftover food out of the oven and buttered the bread at the kitchen worktop.

'The incident room phone line has gone crazy,' Kate picked up, after a deep sigh. 'The usual cranks are giving it their best shot. I've got a team staffing the phone line overnight. We'll sift through the calls in the morning.'

'Have you had time to read your dad's notebook properly yet?' Charlotte asked.

'No, not yet. I've flicked through it, but it's handwritten. Dad wasn't the tidiest writer. A lot of it is disjointed notes, too. I'll give it another go tonight, once the kids are in bed.'

Will delivered the sandwich, which Kate took a large bite out of.

'There's nothing quite like a fish finger sandwich on buttered white bread,' she remarked. 'Thanks, Will, that'll save me putting on a ready-meal when I get home.'

'I'll leave you two ladies to it,' Will said, heading through to the lounge.

'So, what did you want to chat about?' Charlotte asked once he'd gone.

'I need to ask a favour,' Kate began, after finishing her mouthful of food. 'It's probably just as well Will isn't around when I ask you this.'

'Oh, do tell,' Charlotte said, excited by the prospect of something that didn't entail lying in bed all day.

'We telephoned Jimmy Rylands' mobile number this afternoon. The one you passed on from Casey—'

'Brilliant. Did you speak to him?'

'Yes. But only for a moment. He won't speak to the police—'

'Damn.'

'—but he will speak to you.'

'Oh shit. Really? Why?'

'He reckons we'll stitch him up. He's right, we will if we can. He doesn't like you at all, he's so pissed off you got away when he tried to kill you. I think he's come to respect you, though. Anyway, he'll only speak to you.'

'Anything on Casey?'

'Yes, he has Casey—'

'Fuck. Is she okay?'

'Yes, he assures me she's fine. He won't tell me what he wants with her. He says all will be revealed when he speaks to you. You're the go-between. I don't know what he's got planned, but this feels like he's setting up some sort of grand finale. I get a bad feeling about it.'

'If it helps Casey, I'll do whatever I can. Poor Casey. She must be terrified. At least we know why he's interested in her now. She must know something she hasn't told us.'

'That's what I think,' Kate agreed. 'Whatever the hell is going on between all these people, I think we're going to get some answers soon. I'm just concerned that we'll lose more lives before we get there.'

'What do you want me to do?' Charlotte asked.

'Call him,' Kate replied, reaching into her pocket.

'Now?'

'Yes, please. We can't leave this. Think of Casey. He has her somewhere. We need to find her. We know how crazy this guy is.'

'Do your bosses know about this?'

'DSU Pickering agreed to it. It's on a need-to-know basis.'

Kate dropped a piece of paper on the table. A mobile phone number was scrawled on it.

Charlotte pulled her phone out of her back pocket and started to dial.

'Don't get personal with him,' Kate warned. 'Keep it businesslike and simple.'

Charlotte's palms were sweaty. She placed the phone on speaker so Kate could hear what was going on. The call was picked up.

'Yes.'

'It's Charlotte Grayson. You wanted me to call.'

'Are you alone?' he asked.

Charlotte looked at Kate, who nodded.

'Yes.'

'Hello, DCI Summers? Do you think I'm stupid? I saw you on the TV earlier. You think you have me, but you're still a million miles away. Be patient, you'll soon find out what this is about. And, when you do, you cops will have egg all over your faces.'

Kate said nothing. Instead, she encouraged Charlotte to continue.

'What can I do?' she asked.

'Midday. Tomorrow. Cockersand Abbey. Meet me there. Alone. I have Gogs - Casey. She's safe - for now. If you bring cops, you'll never find where Casey is hidden. Just you and me alone, okay. I won't hurt you, I just want to talk. Okay?'

Charlotte looked at Kate again, who paused a moment, then nodded.

'Okay. I'll see you there. Midday.'

There was a pause at the end of the line.

'I know you're listening, DCI Summers. I mean it. If you, or any of your cop friends, turn up, Casey gets it. I'll disappear into the night, and you'll never know what the fuck this is all about. If you play it my way, you'll finally get to find out how your dad died.'

TWENTY-THREE

'I can't believe I'm doing this,' Charlotte said, as she sat at the table with Will, ready to watch Milo's live stream from wherever it was in Morecambe he was broadcasting from. She'd discussed Kate's proposal with him the previous night. He was dead against it, and it was only when Kate reassured him of the safety measures that would be in place that he reluctantly agreed.

'We can't just leave Casey at his mercy,' Charlotte had pleaded. 'What if that was Lucia?'

'He's probably bluffing,' Will challenged. 'What if he doesn't have Casey? What if Casey is part of this whole goddamn mess?'

'She's part of it,' Kate added. 'But I honestly believe she's a victim, not a killer. I'll monitor Charlotte myself, Will. I would not place her in danger.'

After more than an hour of debate, Will finally agreed to Charlotte meeting with Jimmy Rylands. He insisted Charlotte get a morning check-up from Doctor Henderson to give her the all-clear. It helped that he was out of the way the next day, working at the university for a one-day staff get-together.

'You promise me, the moment it's over, you call me and let me know you're okay.'

'I promise,' Charlotte agreed. 'And, I'm as anxious as you are to get the all-clear from Henderson before I do this.'

She was pleased they'd had it out the night before. She didn't want more bad blood between them. She'd had such a near-miss at the fairground, she needed Will's blessing for what was coming next.

'I'll have to catch the bus soon if you're taking the car today,' Will said, as he finished his toast, 'Hopefully, I'll have time to hear what Milo has to say first.'

'It must be young love, Lucia was up and out of the house with him for 8 o'clock. I haven't seen her out of bed that early in ages.'

Will had the laptop sitting on the table between them, with Milo's live stream channel showing the countdown to when he was going live. The viewer tally was counting up like it was a crazy dial on a digital clock.

'Look, he has thousands of viewers watching,' Charlotte observed. 'More people are watching this than buy the local newspaper each week. No wonder Teddy is struggling to keep the business going.'

'I'll bet Kate is so pissed off with Milo,' Will continued. 'Imagine having a kid like him holding you to account like that. It must rankle her and her superiors.'

'She had a word with him in the dining room last night, after she'd spoken to us. She texted me to let me know. She warned him about his legal obligations and not to withhold information from the police. He assured her he wasn't breaking any rules. Yes, you might say she's pissed off.'

The screen on the live stream page changed from the holding message - *Stand by for the latest revelations, Milonites!* - to a live feed somewhere in Morecambe. Milo was not on the screen yet, and Charlotte and Will tried to figure out where he was. The view was of an open playing area which was located in the middle of what had once been a social housing area.

'That looks like some council estate, but I don't recognise it,' Will started.

'It could be anywhere,' Charlotte added, 'It could be Lancaster, for all we know. I'll bet most of those are privately owned these days; there can't be much social housing left.'

'He doesn't have an audience, yet,' Will continued. 'I wonder where he is.'

Charlotte looked at the small clock at the bottom of the laptop. It was almost 9 o'clock.

Milo appeared on the screen.

'Greetings, Milonites!' he started. 'I'm Internet Sleuth Milo De Vries, and today, I'm unearthing more deceptions in Morecambe, this time on this housing estate in Westgate—'

Charlotte picked up her phone and entered the name of the estate in Google Maps.

'He's here, I reckon,' she showed Will, pointing at her screen. 'There's a play area there. I don't know anything about it, do you?'

Will shrugged. Milo continued with his introduction.

'As you know, twenty-five years ago, four school children lost their freedom in this northern seaside resort after being found guilty of murdering their teacher—'

'Come on, Milo, we know this already,' Charlotte spoke at the laptop screen.

'At half-past nine today, I'm going to reveal the two

houses on this estate which are at the centre of what went on that terrible night. If you're a Milonite, and you want to join me, I'd love to meet you on the green here, and say hello. Keep listening, Milonites. All will be revealed!'

'The damn tease,' Will cursed. 'I'm going to have to get my bus now. I'll try and watch it en route if the wireless signal holds. Where are my headphones?'

Charlotte looked at the live feed which had now returned to an open view of the green. At one point, she saw Lucia walk in front of the camera, and there were already excited voices in the background as people from the estate began to gather to see what was going on.

'This guy is amazing,' Charlotte remarked. 'Imagine the confidence it takes to do something like that. My initial scepticism is rapidly turning into begrudging and curmudgeonly respect.'

Will laughed as he wrapped up his headphone lead, stuffed his wallet in his pocket and walked over to kiss Charlotte.

'Promise me you'll play it safe today, Charlotte.'

'I promise.'

She held his gaze in order to give it her best shot at reassuring him.

'Okay, I still don't believe you, but I have to trust you, I suppose. I love you. Call me as soon as it's over.'

Will gave her a second kiss and left to catch his bus. Charlotte was at a loose end now. She didn't want to shower yet or do something else, in case she missed any updates from Milo.

Kate had texted her, equally annoyed at the delay.

WTF? Come on Milo, I haven't got all day!

Charlotte moved the cups and plates over to the sink and ran the tap into the washing bowl. Over the sound of running water, she heard shouting coming through the speaker on the laptop. She shook her hands dry, wiped them on the tea towel, and rushed back to the table.

An altercation was going on. She could hear shouting and screaming, but it was off-camera. One of those screams was Lucia's.

'What the hell?' she said aloud.

The camera shook, then somebody grabbed the camera and tripod. The image blurred for a few seconds as the video feed swept across the grass, panned along the houses in the distance, then settled on a scene which made Charlotte's legs give way. She clutched the side of a chair and sat down before she fell.

There on the screen, holding Milo's phone like he was taking a selfie, was the man they knew as Jimmy Rylands. The arm that wasn't holding the tripod-mounted camera was wrapped around her daughter's neck, and he was clutching a large, oily screwdriver in it. The metal tip was dangerously close to Lucia's eyes.

'Get on the back of the bike, dickhead!' Rylands yelled. 'Do it now or your girlfriend's lovely eyes get gouged out.'

Milo's calm voice could be heard off-camera.

'It's okay, Lucia, I'm not going to let him hurt you. Stay calm. I'm going to do exactly what you say. I'll walk over to the motorcycle now—'

'Get on the back. Do it now!'

Rylands looked crazy. The crowd was growing in bravado, urging him to leave Lucia alone.

'That's not cool. Leave her alone.'

'She's just a kid. Fuck off, why don't you?'

Jimmy seemed more desperate every time someone had a go at him. Charlotte could only look and wait, her heart in suspended animation, her eyes trained on the terrified, white face of her daughter.

The camera pointed at the floor, and Charlotte heard a scream from Lucia. There was a tussle, but she couldn't see anything. Milo's camera was all over the place. Then, there was the sound of a motorcycle revving and Jimmy Ryland's voice screaming directly into the microphone of Milo's phone, so close that it distorted.

'You fuckers want to know what went on here twenty-five years ago. I'll tell you. I'll tell you everything. And, it's not what you think. Six o'clock tonight on this prick's live stream. You'll finally know what the fuck went on that night when David Brewer died.'

TWENTY-FOUR

Morecambe, 1996

Frank had drawn the long straw. He'd been assigned to a town centre beat patch, on his own, and the residents of Morecambe were obliging him by staying on their best behaviour. The weather was fair, and the biting wind that often came off the bay had decided to give them all a break.

It was the kind of day Frank relished as a beat officer, a chance to walk through the town centre, chat to the locals and engage in a good bit of community policing. If he could do this all the time, working 9-5, it would suit him just fine. Unfortunately, the criminal fraternity didn't keep to office hours, which meant shift work was an occupational hazard. Hence, the impending move to detective.

Frank entered the Arndale Centre and took a good look around. It was packed with retirees and parents with toddlers. The shopping centre was filled with a gentle hubbub, everybody was going about their business and staying out of each others' way. Even the police radio was quiet; he'd not received an alert all morning.

Shifts like this gave Frank thinking time. The average day could throw up many different interactions; often, connections could be made when he took a step to one side and mulled it all over.

He spotted an empty chair at a bakery so checked in with Control and signed himself out for a lunch break. Moments later, he was enjoying a meat pasty and a cup of tea, wondering how he could move on matters with the motorcycle campaign. They weren't making much progress, and it needed a different approach. He just couldn't think what it was.

As he sat at the table enjoying his pasty, he stared at the passers-by. He could see that school children were starting to appear, signalling that it must be lunchtime at the local comprehensive. This wasn't too much of a problem from a policing point-of-view, it was mainly sixth-formers and kids who had permission to be in town, nothing that would cause any trouble.

The Arndale Centre had circular, wooden-slatted seating areas dotted along the main thoroughfare, and his attention was caught by a young girl who had just sat down there. He thought he recognised her, but was unable to place her. Her eyes were red; she'd been crying.

Frank watched as she took her glasses out of her pocket. They were thick and heavy. He knew this girl. It was Casey, the kid they all called Gogs or Goggles.

Frank took a sip of his tea. He didn't want to intervene just yet; he was more interested in getting a feel for what was going on. The girl wiped her eyes with a handkerchief and continued to sit there, composing herself. For all Frank knew, it was boyfriend trouble. He knew enough from his awkward conversations with Kate that teenage girls and their romantic relationships were treacherous territory. He had no desire to tempt fate if this was just some trivial matter.

He returned to his pasty, resolving to check in on Jonny Irving if he could find the time. He needed to follow up on the Heysham Moss incident. He was reluctant to sign this over to another PC; Irving was a man he wanted to keep his eye on.

When he looked up again, a sturdily built man was standing over Casey as she remained seated. He was broad-shouldered and fit, wearing a tracksuit and carrying a plastic bag from a supermarket.

Frank's legs tensed, expecting it to be Jonny Irving. He realised he was wrong when the man turned to the side as he was talking to her. He tried to place him. He'd seen him at the school and sometimes in the local paper, alongside sports teams. The body language was awkward, but not hostile. He watched and waited a while.

Casey seemed uncomfortable and embarrassed, the man persistent, but not threatening. Frank realised who it was: David Brewer, one of the teachers at the school. He was a bit of a prima donna as far as he could tell. He wasn't sure if he'd taught his kids.

Brewer sat next to Casey, and she squirmed a little. She wasn't making an attempt to run away, and Brewer wasn't restraining her, so Frank let it play out. If he waded in with his big policing boots and intruded on some private teacher and pupil conversation, it would make him seem like an amateur among his colleagues.

He finished off his pasty and drink, then walked over to the counter to pay his bill. As he turned, he saw a red-faced Brewer walking away, a look of thunder on his face, and Casey removing her glasses once again to wipe the tears from her eyes.

'Keep the change,' he said to the counter assistant and exited the shop. As Brewer was well on his way, he headed directly for Casey.

'Hi, Casey. Remember me? I'm PC Allan.'

Casey sniffed, wiped her eyes with her hands and replaced her glasses.

'Hi, PC Allan.'

'Are you alright, Casey?'

'I'm fine, PC Allan. I just came into town to get a fitting for my new contact lenses. It's just that I ran into Mr Irving again on my way into town—'

'Has he been bothering you again? Have you spoken to your parents about him?'

'He keeps asking me about my dad's work. He's so creepy. He says horrible things—'

'Where does your dad work, Casey?'

'At the betting shop in the West End. I don't know why he keeps asking about that. And, he keeps telling me how pretty I am without my glasses. And, asking me to cuddle him. It's horrible.'

'Have you told your mum and dad?' Frank asked again.

'I don't want to cause trouble for Seth and Josh. I just want him to stop it. I'll try and avoid him, I'm sure he'll get fed up after a while.'

'Why was that teacher speaking to you?'

'That was Mr Brewer. He saw me arguing with Seth's dad and came to see if I was okay—'

'Is he your teacher?'

'No, but he's a team leader at ATC; I know him from there.'

Frank paused a moment, considering whether to push her further. It seemed to him that Casey had already had her fair share of problems with adult men for one day.

'You seemed upset when he left. Did he say or do anything that upset you?'

Casey paused before answering.

'He told me I should report Mr Irving to the police. He threatened to tell my parents about it. He said he has a duty of care or something like that. He told me he can't turn a blind eye to it if I'm in trouble.'

'Is that why he looked so angry?' Frank asked.

'He got angry because I told him to get lost. It's up to me to sort this out. I don't want to mess things up for Seth and Josh. They don't want to go into a home. Seth will be old enough to take care of his brother and sister soon. He just has to hang on until he's eighteen—'

Casey broke down in tears. She was crying so much now, she'd given up on leaving her spectacles on.

'I said a terrible thing—' Casey wept. 'I'm sorry, PC Allan, but I didn't want him to tell.'

'What did you say, Casey?'

'I said I'd tell everybody he was a paedophile if he spoke to my parents. I'm sorry, PC Allan, but I had to do something to stop him telling.'

TWENTY-FIVE

Charlotte couldn't care less if she was still wearing pyjamas. She picked up her phone and the car keys and ran out of the building to the car. She met Will making his way home on the way.

'You saw that, too?' he asked, out of breath.

'Yes. You take the keys and drive, I'll text Lucia to make sure she's okay—'

They climbed into the car; Will started the engine before Charlotte's door was closed. There were no references made to the condition of her health this time around.

Kate had texted.

FFS! We're heading over there now. So sorry about Lucia. Will update you.

There was no update from Lucia. Charlotte had Jimmy's mobile number. She'd called from her phone the previous evening. She redialled from her recent calls menu. It rang several times, then went to voicemail. There was no bespoke welcome, it just switched to the default service. Charlotte was sure as hell leaving a message.

'You piece of shit! Do you know how young my

daughter is? If you harm either Casey or Milo, I will hunt you down and beat the shit out of you—'

The recording locked out, and she was asked if she wished to check her message or record it again by the automated voice. Will laughed.

'What the hell are you laughing for?' she yelled at Will.

'Woah, steady. I'm sorry, you just made me laugh. You sounded like Liam Neeson on the phone there. You'll be telling him you have a particular set of skills next—'

'I do have a particular set of skills. It's called being a mum. I kick the arse of anybody who dares threaten my children - can't you drive any faster?'

'Come on Charlotte, I have to stick to the limit. We're almost there. Anything from Lucia? Check my phone, too—'

He handed it over. Charlotte keyed in Will's code and looked for messages.

I'm OK. L x

Charlotte's phone vibrated, too. Lucia had sent her the same message.

'Here's the estate,' Will said, signalling to turn off the road. 'It should be along here somewhere.'

A crowd was already gathered at the green, and two police vehicles, blue lights flashing, were on the scene. Will pulled the car up at the first space available, and the two of them leapt out, not bothering to close their doors. Lucia was with a WPC, looking shaken.

'Lucia, we're here now,' Charlotte began.

'Do you know these people?' the WPC asked, immediately on her guard.

'Yes,' Lucia replied, looking like a child whose parents had just come to comfort them after a nightmare. 'It's my mum and dad. You might have put some clothes on, Mum—'

'We left in a bit of a rush,' Charlotte answered, wrapping her arms around her daughter.

'What happened, Lucia?' Will asked, kissing her on her head.

'This crazy guy pulled up on a motorbike, marched up to Milo, grabbed me around the neck, and then, took Milo's tripod and camera. I'm so scared about Milo. Will he hurt him, Mum?'

Kate Summers had arrived. She walked directly up to the family. Charlotte's phone vibrated again. It was Olli, checking in on his sister. Charlotte responded with a quick holding message.

She's OK. Talk soon. Mum x

'Are you alright, Lucia? Did he hurt you?'

'I'm fine, Kate. But what about Milo?'

Lucia's voice was desperate.

'We've got all units looking out for him. He was last spotted on Westgate; we've got eyes all over now.'

'Will he be hurt?' Lucia asked.

'I don't think so, Lucia. Did he take Milo's phone?'

'Yes, he did.'

'I think he plans to broadcast via Milo's channel this evening, just in time for the evening news programmes. I don't know what his endgame is. He has some sort of grudge and wants to get his grievance heard. I think he'll do that tonight; we have until then to apprehend him—'

She looked at Charlotte who gave her head a small shake. She didn't want Lucia to know what she was planning to do at midday.

'We'll find him, Lucia. We're getting the police helicopter mobilized; we can use drones, too, if we think we know where he is. He'll be cornered soon enough—'

'But, what happens when he is cornered?' Lucia challenged her. 'He's likely to do something desperate then, isn't he? You remember Edward Callow, he was crazy when he thought his time was up.'

Kate looked at Will and Charlotte before answering.

'It's okay, Kate, you don't have to sugar coat it,' Will reassured her.

'You're an intelligent girl, Lucia. You've seen how these people operate. He knows we know his identity now, so he has very little to lose. We've already messed up his game plan because he failed to kill Seth Irving or any of the other children. In fact, he's made a bit of a mess of the whole thing. We have to get to him before he makes that broadcast this evening. After he's done that, I think he'll be happy to see the world burn around him.'

'You have to go at midday,' Will said, quietly.

'What?' Kate and Charlotte asked at the same time.

'I get it now. I can see how this works. Lucia was just minding her business, giving Milo a hand. Her only crime was being his girlfriend and in the wrong place at the wrong time. I get it, Charlotte. Do what you have to do. You have my blessing now. But you make sure you keep her safe, Kate, okay?'

'What's he talking about, Mum?' Lucia asked.

'I'm seeing this man at midday,' Charlotte explained. 'I take it you're going to try and take him down then, Kate?'

'We are, but only once you're safely out of the way,' Kate confirmed.

'Make sure you get the fucker,' Lucia implored. 'And give him a kick in the bollocks for me, if you do.'

Nigel turned up just as Charlotte realised she'd received a voicemail while she'd been talking. She keyed in her PIN and listened.

'Ha-ha, think you're a tough guy, eh, Charlotte?'

It was Jimmy Rylands, a sneering tone in his voice.

'I've got your gayboy, Milo, with me right now. He and Casey are getting acquainted with each other. Milo's getting the exclusive; he already knows why Casey Gogarty is here. Make sure you're at Cockersand Abbey at midday. I need one last thing from you. Any cops, and it's game over for your pals.'

Charlotte interrupted Kate who was getting Lucia to run through what had happened once again. She played the message on speakerphone.

Kate shook her head.

'I'm no psychologist, Charlotte, but this seems to be heading for one dramatic climax. I'm concerned about what's planned for the fireworks. This is the kind of nutter who shoots himself afterwards. The trouble is, they always take innocent people down with them. Don't share this with Lucia, but I am concerned. We're getting armed officers deployed. I think this is going to be serious if we can't defuse it.'

'That makes me feel better about midday,' Charlotte answered. 'You don't think he'll try and take me too, do you?'

'No,' Kate replied with certainty. 'My guess is that he now has a begrudging respect for you. You're also a trusted conduit between him and the police. And, you know Casey and Milo. I think you're the go-between, he has no interest in kidnapping you. I don't think he likes you very much, but he has hostages if that's what he wants. He has his leverage if we find where he's hiding.'

'Well, that makes me feel slightly better—'

'Nice to see you came dressed for the occasion,' Nigel teased as he joined the two women after chatting to Will and Lucia. 'I hope I haven't caught you in any of my photographs. I'm not sure what Teddy would say about one of his reporters attending a crime scene in their nightwear.'

Kate and Charlotte laughed. Charlotte had left the house in such a rush, she'd still got her slippers on. Jimmy Rylands had caught her on the hop one too many times. The next time they met, she'd be ready for him.

TWENTY-SIX

Doctor Henderson finished his examination of Charlotte and placed his medical equipment back in his bag.

'I think it's all that running you do. You shouldn't be as well as you are, but it's looking good, Charlotte. I want you to take things easy still. But, you're fine if you go gently.'

That was exactly the news she wanted. Since watching Lucia threatened on Milo's live feed, Charlotte's heart was on fire. Not with the pain or discomfort from her electric shock, but fuelled by the frustration and anger that had got her into trouble before. These guys thought they could get away with it every time. They harassed and intimidated with impunity. It infuriated her, and she would do whatever she could to get this madman locked up.

As she rolled down her sleeve, she felt her phone buzz in her pocket. She took it out and checked. Will's day at the university had been rapidly rescheduled. He'd taken Lucia for a check-up at the infirmary. He'd used the family car for transport. The message on her phone confirmed that all was well.

Lucia was shaken but not stirred. Will x

'So, you didn't think of letting me take care of your daughter's medical needs?' Henderson smiled at her.

'Ha, no, I thought we'd better not get used to your off-the-books services. It's not that I don't trust you. You've worked wonders for me. I just figured she'd best go to the infirmary as the police were officially involved in this latest altercation.'

'I reckon I could make my living patching up you and your family,' Henderson continued. 'There's plenty of work there to keep one man busy.'

Charlotte laughed.

'Seriously, Doctor Henderson, you, me and Will are quits now. You've done more than enough. The threat of torture is forgiven. Your soul is cleansed. At least, as far as I'm concerned.'

She spotted a tear in his eye.

'That means more than you'll ever know,' he said. 'All I ever wanted to do was to heal people.'

Charlotte was mindful of the time. Kate would be waiting outside for her shortly. She finished with the doctor and walked down the stairs with him.

'I'll call in tomorrow, but just call me if you need anything. Any time. I mean that.'

As Charlotte watched him walking along the path, Kate drew up in her car and gave a wave. She wound down her window to exchange a few words with the doctor.

'Ready for this?' she said to Charlotte as she reached the vehicle.

'As ready as I'll ever be,' Charlotte replied.

'I have a team at Cockersand Abbey right now preparing the area. We have plainclothes officers pretending to be walkers, we've got armed officers on standby in the old farmhouse nearby, and I'll be in earpiece contact with you throughout. We're not wiring you. We're going to put a Bluetooth device in your ear and communicate over a mobile phone, in case he checks you first. How does that sound?'

Kate started the car.

'I'm trusting you to get it right,' Charlotte replied. The thought of armed officers scared the life out of her. When Edward Callow was threatening her and Lucia with a gun, they turned up unannounced. It was more nerve-wracking knowing they'd have their weapons trained on Jimmy Rylands.

'Will they just shoot him?' Charlotte asked. She hadn't a clue how these things worked.

'No,' Kate replied. 'Only if he draws a gun. Or, if your life is in immediate danger. But that's not his way of working. I'd be less surprised if this guy turned up with a flame thrower. Fortunately, guns don't seem to be his thing.'

'We're heading in the wrong direction, aren't we?' Charlotte asked, wondering why Kate had just driven past a turnoff.

'Yes, we're dropping in on Seth and Josh first. Josh called me; they've got a problem over at the holiday lodge.'

Kate ran through the details of the operation several times on the drive over. Charlotte fixed it in her mind. As far as she could tell, it was as safe as it could be.

'I'm certain he's going to ask you for something,' Kate said as they pulled into the caravan park. 'He'll make some unreasonable demand. Probably money and anonymity. Just tell him you'll speak to me, and assure him that you'll do your best to secure it. I don't want anything placed in his way. If we frustrate him, he'll only get madder.'

'That's good to know,' Charlotte replied, unbuckling her seatbelt.

'One moment,' Kate said. 'I told Josh I'd warn him when we're here.'

She took out her phone and sent a text message.

'Okay, we're clear.'

The two women walked along the network of asphalt roads to Josh's lodge. He saw them from the window and opened the door to them.

'Everything alright, Josh?' Kate asked. 'You look worried.'

'Seth has gone missing—' Josh began.

'Oh, for Christ's sake,' Kate cursed. 'When?'

'An hour ago,' Josh continued.

'Any idea why?'

'I've got a pretty good idea, DCI Summers,' a different voice replied.

Charlotte gasped as Eric Bennett walked out of the hallway and into the living area.

'Eric. What the hell are you doing here?'

Kate took the words out of Charlotte's mouth.

'I followed you the other day when you drove out here—'

'I didn't see you—' Kate protested.

'That's kind of the whole point,' Eric smiled.

'Seth has taken my mountain bike,' Josh added. 'He took the keys to my storage area and climbed out the back window of the lodge. It was a half-hour before we realised that he'd gone.'

'Not the car?' Kate asked.

Josh gave her a look.

'Seth can't drive. He rode motorcycles before he was convicted, and he's been preoccupied for the last twenty-five years, unless you'd forgotten that?'

Kate apologized, and Charlotte spared her further embarrassment by changing the subject.

'Why are you even here, Eric? You know Josh's identity is supposed to be confidential.'

Charlotte noticed that Kate was also struggling to make any sense of all this. 'I wanted to see the guys,' Eric replied. 'And, I saw that live stream this morning. Everybody saw that live stream this morning. I decided it's time for us all to talk.'

'You know he has Gogs, don't you?' Charlotte asked.

Both men looked at her. There was her answer. They didn't know.

'He has Gogs? You mean he's kidnapped her?' Josh asked.

'Yes. He's got some big revelation planned for six o'clock tonight,' Kate said, pausing a moment after she spoke. 'I shouldn't be telling you this, but we're on our way to try to apprehend him now—'

'You know where he is?' Eric asked.

'He wants to speak to me,' Charlotte answered.

'Can we come?' Josh said. 'Maybe we can identify this guy. Perhaps it's Robbie—'

'It's not Robbie,' Kate asserted, a little more forcefully than she should have. 'He calls himself Jimmy Rylands—'

'Jimmy Rylands? He was a kid from school, wasn't he?'

Eric looked at Josh as he spoke.

'Yes, a creepy kid if I remember. Younger than us. Always messing around with lighters at smoker's corner. I never saw the kid smoke a cigarette. All he did every break was play with cigarette lighters and burn cigarette papers. That's him, isn't it?'

'Why is he caught up in this?' Eric continued. 'He had nothing to do with what went on back then. He was just one of those kids who was around. Though, come to think of it, didn't his mum know your dad, Josh?'

'My dad knew lots of women around Morecambe. God only knows what they saw in him. I think that's why mum left in the end; she'd had enough of his drinking and womanising.'

'Did you manage to track the mother down?' Charlotte asked.

Kate shook her head.

'Only kind of. She moved to Spain over a decade ago. We're trying to trace her through the Spanish police. It'll take some time.'

'So, who is this guy?' Charlotte spoke aloud, summing up the thoughts of everybody in the room. 'And, why does he even care what went on twenty-five years ago?'

TWENTY-SEVEN

Morecambe, 1996

Frank Allan didn't particularly relish the thought of a parents' evening at the school, but he accepted that this was one of the jobs which came in the parenting handbook. Just like ferrying youngsters between weekend sporting fixtures, hosting birthday parties for over-excited and sugar-fuelled kids, and combing headlice out of his daughter's long hair when she was at primary school, it was another one of those thankless tasks which just had to be done.

It wasn't that he was disinterested in the academic progress of his children. He was completely engaged in how they were getting on at school and faring in their studies. It was just that parents' evenings were a particular kind of torture contrived to torment all parents. It was even worse if you had more than one child.

Frank was shuffling on an uncomfortable plastic seat in the school's main hall, next to a parent who was doing her best to entertain a grouchy toddler who should have been in bed an hour previously. Frank was running twenty minutes behind schedule. He'd got caught behind a pushy couple who insisted on over-running their ten-minute slot. Their self-centredness meant that everybody who was in that teacher's orbit was now ten minutes off their schedule. It only took a couple of instances like that, and the whole system went awry.

Frank couldn't figure out why the school insisted on adhering to an appointments system. In his view, they should have sounded a bell every ten minutes - like a boxing match - and signalled that a slot was over, no arguments. Alternatively, the teachers should have accepted that it always descended into chaos, and let the parents passive-aggressively sort it out between themselves.

He was growing impatient, as he always did at these events. He didn't want to feel that way, it was his two kids he was there for after all, but it always played out the same way. It didn't help that the toddler was irritable and moaning, but he was stuck with it until the teacher became free for his appointment.

As Frank sat there, he cast his gaze around the room to see if he knew any of the other parents. Evie had spared him this ordeal when she was alive, briefing him and the kids on everything that the teachers had told her. He knew more locals through his policing work than as a parent, but that situation was changing fast since he'd been sole carer for the kids.

He scanned the hall. Some of the parents had brought their children with them. Frank preferred not to do that. He wanted the teachers to be able to speak freely. How else would he know if any problems were lurking?

One of the children who was accompanied by her parents was Casey Gogarty. She was with her mum and dad. She seemed happier than she had done when he'd seen her in the Arndale Centre. He resolved to try and catch her with her parents and have a casual exchange, just to check the lie of the land.

He also spotted David Brewer holding court at a table, accompanied by a younger teacher who he hadn't seen before. Brewer was clearly in charge, the other man looked like he was an apprentice or newly-qualified teacher, perhaps learning the ropes. Frank noted as Brewer worked through the queuing parents that he dispatched them swiftly. Also, none of the children attended his sessions.

At last, it was Frank's turn with the history teacher. She apologised for running late, gave Frank a glowing account of Brett's performance and reassured him that there were no signs that Brett was struggling after the death of his mum. That was really what Frank was there to hear. So long as they were managing to adjust to life without their mum, and not going off the rails at school, that was better than he might have hoped for.

Frank thanked the teacher, freed up the uncomfortable plastic seat for the parent with the ill-tempered child, and examined his list for the next destination. He looked about the room for the geography teacher. There was a long line of parents formed in front of his desk; it was time to depart from his list and snatch the appointments wherever he found a free teacher. Before doing that, he wanted a cup of tea from the canteen, where they were serving refreshments. Frank wasn't much of a drinker, but he reckoned they'd give school funds a huge boost if they opened up an alcoholic bar on parents' evenings.

He joined the line for a cup of tea. The man who he assumed to be Casey Gogarty's dad was directly in front of him. He might have been frustrated in his parental role, but here was an opportunity to do a bit of policing work.

'Have you got many more teachers to see?' he asked, opting for the polite chit-chat approach. It was a well-known strategy for a beat bobby.

'Only three more, and we're out of here,' the man replied. 'I need a strong coffee; these evenings are not for the faint-hearted, are they?'

Frank smiled. He seemed like a perfectly likable guy.

'Are you here directly from work?' Frank asked.

'Yes, though I'm lucky, I can get away early. I work in a bookies. Once the afternoon races are finished and the punters have claimed on their betting slips, we're done. Except for the counting up and banking, of course. But that can wait until tomorrow.'

'You keep cash on the premises?' Frank wondered, aloud. 'Sorry, I'm Frank Allan. I'm a local copper. I'm not planning to rob your premises, honestly.'

The man laughed.

'You don't look the sort to go robbing shops. But yes, sometimes we have to leave cash on the premises. It's in a safe. Why, do you think that's asking for trouble?'

'No, no, not at all. But do me a favour, will you? Just take a little extra care over the next couple of weeks. We've had a spate of near misses in the resort. I'd hate you to lose your takings to some ne'er-do-well.'

It was a harmless lie, but Frank got a nasty feeling about Jonny Irving, and he'd have kicked himself if he didn't say something to Casey's dad.

'I'll pop in some time when I get a minute. I can give the premises the once-over and perhaps offer some basic security advice. It's all part of the service. I'll be in uniform then, I'll have my ID on me, you'll know I'm not casing out the joint.'

The man laughed and picked up his drinks.

'Nice to meet you, Frank. I'll look forward to seeing you again.'

Frank placed his order at the cafeteria and looked around the hall again. Brewer had left his desk, which was now manned by the younger teacher, although no parents were waiting in their queue. Casey's dad had just joined her mum, who'd succeeded in finding a free teacher. Casey was no longer with them.

His tea arrived, so he paid and walked over to the stage at the front of the hall and sat on the edge. He placed his drink at his side and looked around for Brewer. He was tall and easy to spot. Frank saw him by the double doors at the far side of the hall. He was speaking to Casey. Although there were no raised voices, they looked tense and awkward. Casey stormed off, tears in her eyes. She exited the hall, making her way out into the reception area. Brewer looked flustered and annoyed. Casey's parents had missed every-thing; they were deep in conversation with the teacher.

Frank stood up and walked toward Brewer. Whatever was going on between these two, he wanted to know. Brewer was heading directly for him.

'Mr Brewer?' Frank asked. 'David Brewer?'

Brewer stopped and looked at Frank, trying to figure out if he knew him.

'I'm Frank Allan, Kate and Brett's dad.'

His face was blank. It was a big school, there was no reason why he'd know the kids if he hadn't taught them.

Brewer was curt and abrupt; it rubbed Frank up the wrong way.

'Might I have a quiet word?' Frank asked. 'It's about that young lady you were just speaking to—'

Frank kept his voice quiet, he didn't want to cause Brewer any embarrassment.

'Why, what do you want to know? What's she been saying?'

Brewer was immediately defensive. He was speaking louder than was appropriate in such a public space.

'It's nothing serious, Mr Brewer; maybe we can have a quiet word outside—'

Brewer's voice was raised like he was addressing a class full of children.

'No, Mr Allan, we can not have a quiet word outside. If you wish to speak to me, make an appointment or ask to speak to the headteacher. In the meantime, I'd be grateful if you left me alone.'

The entire school hall quietened as he put Frank in his place. Brewer's face was red.

'Carry on everybody, there's nothing to see here,' he shouted like he was splitting up a fight in the playground.

After a few moments, the chatter continued, and Frank was left standing in the middle of the room feeling stupid and humiliated. Brewer had got the better of him this time; he was on his own territory, there was nothing Frank could do at that moment. But he sure as hell was keeping an eye on Brewer. He didn't like the man, and if he was bothering Casey, he'd better keep a lookout. If there was one thing Frank Allan hated as a cop, it was a bully. And, Brewer was a bully.

TWENTY-EIGHT

Charlotte was more nervous than she had felt for some time. Kate's team had taken over a vacant static caravan close to Cockerham Sands, and the Bluetooth was being set up on her phone so that it connected with a small earpiece. A detective constable asked Charlotte to place it in her ear, then adjusted her hair so that her ears were properly covered.

'Right, your phone is charged, the Bluetooth is working, you've used your phone at the abbey before, so you know you can get a signal out there. We're good to go, I think. We'll just run a test with DCI Summers when she's available. If he's armed, or if you feel in any danger, the code word is Sunderland Point. If we hear that, officers will come to help you immediately.'

Charlotte thanked the officer and adjusted her hair so that it sat more comfortably. Kate walked into the static caravan. Her face showed the tension that was in the air.

'Shooters are in place at the farmhouse, ma'am,' another officer confirmed with her. 'Mrs Grayson needs to stay at the back of the building for direct line of sight.'

'Did you hear that, Charlotte?' Kate checked. 'If you give the code word, drop to the floor, and let the firearms team do their thing. Oh, and close your eyes. It will be fast and clean, but you won't want to see it—'

'You sound like you're expecting to take him down,' Charlotte said, concerned at the presence of guns, even in the most capable hands.

'No, I'm not expecting to have to shoot him. This isn't the Wild West; we have specific rules of engagement in this country. He's not a terrorist either, so we can't just shoot him if he starts sounding off. But, if we do have to shoot - say, he has a gun - then we shoot to kill, not to wound. You need to understand that.'

'Okay, let's just hope he's not an idiot. If he's found himself a gun, I'll be out of there like a shot.'

'Remember, you have officers all around you posing as walkers. The biggest logistical problem is that we can't shut down the area to the public, or we risk alerting him to our presence. That's a pain, we'll just have to hope the wet weather will put people off. And, the fact the tide is due in soon.'

There were too many factors for Charlotte to consider on her own. She knew that the only way through this was to let the police do their job and just get on with her part in the operation. This was going to make an amazing feature for the newspaper, that was for sure.

After getting Kate to take some pictures of her for the article which she was already planning in her mind, one of the detective inspectors called time and announced that everybody needed to take their places.

It was just after half-past eleven. It would take Charlotte ten minutes to walk over to Cockersand Abbey. Nobody knew how Jimmy Rylands would be arriving, but there were officers in unmarked vehicles on watch along the road into Cockerham Sands, ready to apprehend him if he arrived on his stolen motorcycle.

'Good luck,' Kate said, squeezing Charlotte's hand. 'Don't make him angry, just keep him talking, and use the alert words if you feel in danger at any time.'

Charlotte walked out of the static caravan and along the narrow road, past the small parking bay and up to the place where the narrow path to the abbey began. She looked around as she walked, alert for Jimmy, but also trying to figure out who on the beach was a police officer and who was a member of the public. There was nothing that would give the game away as far as she could see.

'Just keep checking in with me on your phone, please,' came Kate's voice in her ear. It was not the most sophisticated of systems, but the simple phone line link worked well. Besides, the police had done well to pull off such a complex operation so quickly.

'I'm hearing you fine,' Charlotte said quietly. 'No problems at this end, though the wind makes it quite difficult to catch what you're saying at times.'

She continued along the path, past the ruin of a barn and through the kissing gate. The shingle to her left rapidly changed to mud and sand, and although the tide was out, she could see that it was beginning to come in. It looked wet and boggy from where she was standing. She was pleased to be able to avoid that area.

Charlotte continued along the path and towards the abbey. She thought back to the last time she'd been there. As far as she could tell, everything looked the same. There was nothing that would alert Jimmy to what was going on.

'No sign of the target yet on the roads or at the abbey,' Kate updated in her earpiece. 'Walk over to the abbey now, and wait at the back of the building where the firearms team can see you. Try to engage him out in the open.'

Charlotte nodded, then remembered Kate would need more than that by way of confirmation. She'd got it into her head that they were monitoring her on video, too. That would have been almost impossible in such a rural location; she was the eyes and ears of the entire operation.

'Will do,' she confirmed.

'Damn!' came Kate's voice in her ear.

'Everything okay there?' Charlotte asked.

'A bloody farmer just turned up on a quad bike. He's fixing a fence or something like that. He's not in the line of sight, but I'd prefer it if he buggered off—'

'Can't you move him on?' Charlotte asked.

'No, it's too late. Jimmy Rylands could be watching already. So long as he sticks to his fence-mending, he'll be fine.'

Charlotte had reached the outer ruins of the abbey now. There was no sign of Jimmy or his motorcycle.

'We're having problems with the wind blowing across the microphone on your mobile phone,' Kate updated her. 'That should resolve when you've got a bit of cover from the abbey; it's so exposed out there.'

'You can say that again,' Charlotte said. 'I hadn't expected it to be such a wet day. I've moved my phone into my inner pocket. Hopefully, that will help.'

'Yes, it's a little muffled, but better out of the wind. Thanks, Charlotte.'

'Okay, I'm here. I'm going to shut up now in case he's watching and sees me talking. I don't want to spook him.'

Charlotte circled the edge of the abbey and was surprised to see Herbert Walker's Land Rover parked outside.

'Did you know the stonemason is inside the abbey work-ing?' Charlotte whispered.

'That's why you must engage Jimmy outside. Herbert hasn't moved out of the building all morning. He'll be fine if we leave him be.'

Charlotte wasn't so certain about that. He'd already run into Rylands when Jimmy dropped off flowers there. The two men hadn't exactly hit it off, according to Herbert.

'What's the time?' Charlotte whispered. 'How the hell is he even getting out here?'

'Five minutes to go,' Kate informed her. 'Be patient, I'm sure he'll show. He'll want to make sure you've come alone before he shows his face.'

Charlotte waited outside the rear door, which was still closed, as they'd expected it to be during the hasty planning of the operation. Charlotte looked over to the dilapidated farmhouse across the field. She thought she could see rifles pointing through the smashed windows, but she was imag-ining it; the marksmen had concealed themselves well.

She looked over to her left to see the farmer busying himself with a fence repair. From a distance, he appeared to be completely oblivious to what was going on around him.

Charlotte found a large stone that was big enough to seat her and sat down. If Jimmy Rylands had any intention of turning up, he was taking his time. She just wanted him to show his face so she could get this encounter over and done with.

TWENTY-NINE

'It's ten past twelve, where the fuck is he?'

It was making Charlotte jittery, hearing the tension in Kate's voice. Although Kate wasn't speaking to her, she could hear everything that was being said in the static caravan control centre.

'Any eyes on the target?'

Kate was speaking down the police radio. Charlotte heard the negative replies that came in from the various units.

'I'm going to walk around the abbey, just in case he can't see that I'm here,' Charlotte whispered. 'One slow circuit, that's all.'

'Okay, make sure you return to the line of sight with the farmhouse,' Kate instructed her. 'Stick to the plan, Charlotte. I don't want anybody getting hurt on my watch.'

Charlotte began to circle the abbey, looking all around as she did so. She wouldn't have been surprised if Jimmy had popped up from behind a bush, the way things were going.

The farmer was still busy with some barbed wire,

hammering it into fence posts as far as she could tell from that distance. As she emerged from the side of the abbey, she could see Plover Scar lighthouse in the distance. It looked like a sea of mud out there as far as she could tell; it probably told her everything she needed to know that the dog walkers were avoiding that area. She assumed they were dog walkers. For all she knew, they were undercover officers.

As she came around the front of the abbey, she noticed that the door was ajar, but the cone was not there. Neither was Herbert's keep out message. She stopped outside and listened. She'd expected to hear the tapping of his chisel on the stones, but it was silent. She paused a moment, then recalled Kate's words. *Stick to the plan.*

She was about to continue her circuit of the abbey's exterior when a hand shot out the side of the door and was placed over her mouth. Her heart pounded at the sudden surprise of it. The hand was clammy and smelled of oil. She turned her head and saw Jimmy Rylands inside. He put his finger to his lips using his free hand, and pulled her inside the building.

With his finger still on his lips, he released his hand from her mouth and started to pat her down. He found her phone straight away, taking it out of her pocket. He examined it and saw that a call was active on the screen. He ended the call.

Charlotte let out a gasp.

'Are you going to hurt me?' she asked.

'No,' he replied. 'But I see your uniformed friends are here. Do you think I'm stupid? I knew you wouldn't come alone—'

'How did you get here?' Charlotte asked.

'The stonemason's Land Rover—'

'Is Herbert alright? You didn't hurt him?'

'He should be fine. I dumped him in a barn along one of the country lanes. I'm sure he'll be okay.'

Charlotte could feel her chest tightening. Not only had she lost contact with Kate, but she'd also broken the prime directive; keep him in line of sight of the shooters. Suddenly, she felt all alone.

'Why did you want to see me?' she asked. There was no point in stringing this out. The sooner they got to the point, the better.

'You're a persistent little bitch, aren't you?' Jimmy said. 'How the fuck did you get out of that coffin? And, the electric shock, too. I'm beginning to think you're indestructible—'

'It's because of good luck and good friends,' Charlotte replied. She was about to make a snide comment but held back, recalling Kate's warning to keep him calm.

'Why don't we talk outside?' she suggested.

Jimmy laughed.

'Not a bloody chance. They've got shooters out there. I watched them arriving and setting up. I'm not armed, by the way. You can tell them that on your mobile phone hotline when it's time for me to walk out of here—'

'You can't get away, you know—'

'Well, they can't shoot me without just cause, that's for certain. So, they're going to have to catch me first. Oh, and you can tell your PC Plod friends this too; if they catch me now, Casey and that poncy guy – Milo, whatever his name is - they'll starve and die before they find where I've got them. Let me say what I've got to say this evening, and everybody can walk away.'

'Are Milo and Casey safe?'

'Yes, for now. They're taped up with gaffer tape and

having to piss and shit in a leaky bucket, but other than that, I'd say they're okay.'

'So, what's the plan, Jimmy?' Charlotte asked. 'Why do you want me here?'

'I want safe passage out of the country to Spain—'

'You're joking?'

'No. When you hear what happened that night, you'll see that all I want is justice. Do you think those kids killed David Brewer? Well, they did, but they did something even worse. And, nobody ever knew because nobody gave a shit. Casey Gogarty hasn't told her story yet. Notice how she disappeared from Morecambe and was never seen again? Well, wait until you hear her confession. You'll hear why those kids took the rap for her. She'll be the last to tell their story. And when she speaks, the world will finally know the truth about what happened—'

'But, why do you even care? What's your involvement with all of this?' Charlotte pushed. She could not understand why he was risking so much to reveal his so-called truth. He'd killed two people and injured others. He'd almost killed her, too.

'You'll find out later,' he replied. 'The whole resort will be stunned when they hear the true story. And, that evil bitch, Casey, will get what she deserved all those years back—'

'You're going to hurt her, aren't you?'

Charlotte's mind was racing. Kate had warned her about this. She'd thought he was the kind of psychopath that burned everything down around him. In this case, Jimmy Rylands had previous form.

'Milo De Wanker will get to walk, so long as he helps me live stream Casey's confession. But Casey? I've got something special planned for her. She doesn't walk away from this.'

Charlotte swallowed hard. Poor Casey. Even if she was not innocent of whatever it was Jimmy reckoned she'd done, it was a police matter, not something for a vigilante like him to sort out.

'Okay, why am I here?' she asked. She'd heard enough of his psychotic plans.

'I will spare Casey's life if I'm guaranteed safe passage out of the UK and a pardon. Those people who got killed were accidents—'

'I'm sure that poor tramp would say otherwise—'

'That was a mistake. I thought he was that bastard, Seth. No wonder he wouldn't talk when I hammered his teeth out. He was collateral damage—'

'And Edwin, the funeral director. Herbert? Casey? Milo? Me? Are we all expendable?'

She noticed a look on Jimmy's face which was not dissimilar to Edward Callow's when he was waving a gun at her and Lucia at the top of the freight crane at Heysham Port. He seemed crazed and insane as if he truly believed his delusion and self-justification. He was becoming flustered.

'Look, stop questioning me, okay? I have good reasons for doing what I've done. You'll see. I'll be the hero when you hear Casey's confession. Believe me, you'll see how the cops failed tragically back then.'

'Your mum lives in Spain, doesn't she?'

'You know that?'

'Of course, we do,' Charlotte replied. 'That's where you're heading, isn't it?'

'Yes. When I track her down. The bitch left the country while I was in prison. She'll see that I was right all along. If you know where she is, make sure she's watching the live feed tonight. She'll see how she was wrong all these years.'

At last, here was a clue as to what was driving him. The need to prove something to his mother. A deep sense of injustice and being wronged. But why? Why was this man so angry that he'd risk everything to prove something to his estranged mother?

She was about to ask him more questions when a man walked through the door and caught both of them by surprise. Without hesitation, Jimmy grasped Charlotte around her neck and pulled an oily screwdriver out of his back pocket. Charlotte could see it was the same one he'd used to threaten Lucia earlier. He held it directly over her eyelid. She could feel it scraping the skin, putting pressure on her eyeball.

'Back off, copper or this gets pushed right into her brain.'

THIRTY

Morecambe, 1996

'If you can fetch those leaflets from the car, then we're good to go,' Larry said. They'd just managed to get the gazebo put up without making a pig's ear of it, and they were on a roll.

'Will do,' Frank replied. They'd struck it lucky. The weather was good, and the ATC event seemed a friendly affair. That day's shift was for dedicated outreach work. No domestic rows, no pub drunks or rowdy youths that day. It was a rare opportunity to get out in the community, spread the good word about home security, and see if they could pick up any rumblings which might help them find out who was responsible for the motorcycle thefts.

Due to the age profile of the ATC, it was also the perfect place to let the local youngsters know they were targeting dirt bike riders on public land.

Frank returned with the boxes, and the two men set out their stall of leaflets, posters and stickers. One of the event organisers walked up to them to check everything was going okay.

'Don't I know you?' Frank asked as the young man thanked them for attending.

'I'm a teacher at the school. You don't know me from there, do you?'

Frank realised where he'd seen him before. He was Brewer's mate at the parents' evening. He thought it better to keep his mouth shut after the embarrassing exchange with his teaching friend in the school hall.

'I'm Phil Taylor,' he said, holding out his hand. Frank shook it and said he must be mistaken about knowing the man. It didn't look like Taylor had made the connection. Frank was out of context after all, and in uniform, so Taylor would have been very observant if he had recognised him.

'This is the life,' Larry said, sitting down on one of the beach chairs he'd brought along for their comfort. 'More days like this would be just fine by me.'

The event got busy fast. Phil Taylor seemed caught up in some issue, asking if Frank and Larry knew of any ice cream vendors in the resort. They laughed about that after he'd gone.

'I know Morecambe Police are very flexible,' Frank laughed, 'but sourcing ice cream vendors isn't in our remit last time I looked.'

Before long, their stall was receiving steady customers, though there wasn't much chance of them exposing the motorcycle theft culprits any time soon. The majority of their visitors were kids seeking freebies or parents with toddlers wanting to get a photograph with a policeman.

'And, to think you might be a detective soon,' Larry whispered to Frank. 'We're hardly Starsky and Hutch, are we?'

Frank was distracted. He'd just seen the girl with the heavy spectacles. Casey Gogarty was there, in an ATC uniform, chatting and laughing. She was with the Irving boys. Now there was an unusual match. There were two others there as well. They seemed younger somehow. One was carrying some weight and seemed awkward in his uniform. The other looked like he should have been modelling the uniform in a catalogue, he was so well turned out. It was good to see Casey with youngsters of her own age.

Frank's impulse was to check in on Casey, to make sure things were okay after seeing her upset at the parents' evening. He was about to head over there when Brewer turned up and had a brief exchange with the group. He was dressed in an officer's uniform, like Taylor. The exchange wasn't unfriendly, but Casey didn't look at Brewer through-out, she just stared down, and didn't meet his eye.

Frank was distracted by a couple of children seeking stickers, and he didn't think about it again until he and Larry had a quiet lull.

'I see Rory Higson is here,' Frank observed, 'Looks like he's got the easy job on the newspaper today. We should, perhaps, see if he'll mention the motorcycle campaign. You never know, it might get a slot in this week's paper.'

An ice-cream van arrived to great excitement, and it parked up on the asphalt. The driver had barely put the handbrake on before a queue had formed at the serving hatch.

'Fancy an ice cream?' Larry asked.

'Sure, why not?' Frank replied.

As Larry walked over and joined the queue, Casey passed by, heading for the squadron hut.

'Casey, hi, it's me, Frank Allan.'

She stopped and looked at him like she needed a moment to recall who he was.

'Is everything okay? I wanted to check in with you after our chat in the Arndale Centre the other day—'

'I'm fine, PC Allan, thank you—'

'It's just I saw you talking to Mr Brewer again at the parent's evening. You seemed upset again—'

'Are you following me, PC Allan?'

'No, no, Casey, I'm just concerned about you. If there's anything up, please, talk to your mum and dad or chat to me or my colleague, PC Schofield. That's him over there queuing for ice creams.'

Casey looked over and clocked Larry.

'It's all fine, PC Allan, honestly—'

She looked around and saw something which gave her a start.

'I've got to go, PC Allan. See you.'

She headed off at some speed, checking behind her as she entered the squadron hut.

Frank took a look around to see what had startled her. Jonny Irving was there. He was with a woman and a child.

Frank's immediate impulse was to rush over to Jonny and have the word that he'd been intending to have with him since he'd scared Casey on the motorcycle. Jonny couldn't go around frightening young girls like that. But this was interesting. He was with the same woman that Jonny had been in the pub with when Frank and Larry had had to escort him back to his house. She'd been with Jonny at the fair, too, along with the child. Frank didn't want to cause a scene at a family event.

'Here's your ice cream,' Larry said, handing Frank a 99 cone dripping with chocolate sauce. He took the cone and licked off a drop of ice cream which was just about to fall on his uniform.

'Just watch the stand for a moment, will you, Larry?' he

said. Larry took his seat again underneath the gazebo and set about his ice cream. Frank wasn't in the mood for his anymore. He checked that Larry wasn't watching and dropped it in a bin. He was looking for Jonny.

Frank searched all over, checking the crowd at each stall, hoping to catch a glimpse of Jonny once again. He did his best to stay out of David Brewer's way. All he needed was another run-in with the man at a family event.

Frank had all but given up when he caught sight of Rory Higson watching something behind the bins at the back of the squadron hut. Rory moved on to his car in the car park, but Frank was intrigued to see what had caught his eye. He peered around the side of the squadron hut, not sure what was going to greet him there. It was Jonny Irving, sober and charming, kissing the woman who'd been with him during the pub altercation. It seemed to Frank that Jonny had a new woman in tow. Only, where she figured in the arrangements with his existing family wasn't clear.

THIRTY-ONE

'Okay, I'm stepping back now,' the plain-clothes officer said, calm but cautious. All the time, he held Jimmy in his gaze, alert to any movement which might place Charlotte in danger.

'I said no cops!' Jimmy shouted.

'I thought we'd agreed on this—' Charlotte began, exasperated that an overzealous police officer had just screwed up the rapport she was beginning to build. She'd read about bungled police operations, and this was one of them as far as she was concerned.

'Step well away,' Jimmy instructed, 'I want to see you on the beach, do you understand me?'

'All units stay back,' the officer warned. Charlotte could see he was wearing an earpiece.

'Here's what's going to happen,' Jimmy shouted so that whoever was listening at the other end of the police radio could hear what he was saying. 'I'm going to walk out to that Land Rover using this stupid bitch as a shield. She won't get hurt so long as you keep well away. If I see a twitch from a rifle in that old farmhouse, your annoying friend here loses an eye. I'm going to take that Land Rover and drive out of here. I will release Charlotte Grayson as a sign of goodwill. If you apprehend me now, my two hostages will die of starvation. They're well-hidden and secured, and you will not find them. Charlotte knows what my demands are. Now, you - move!'

Charlotte watched as the officer walked backwards, towards the beach. It was some way off, and after a while, he turned to face his direction of travel as it was too hazardous not to be able to see where he was going.

'Fucking police!' Jimmy cursed. 'They can't stick to a deal—'

'I think they panicked because they couldn't see me—' Charlotte suggested.

'Whatever, I said no cops,' he repeated.

'How about I connect via the phone and reassure them I'm alright? So long as they know I'm not in danger, they'll relax more—'

Jimmy's hand tensed on the screwdriver handle, the point of which was still hovering over her eye. He seemed indecisive for a moment, then released his grip.

'Do it,' he instructed. Charlotte took her phone and dialled Kate.

'Are you okay?' Kate asked before the call was properly connected.

'I'm fine. What the hell was that?'

'I'm sorry. That officer will get a bollocking when this is over. He lost his radio signal for a moment and took the initiative when he saw you going inside the abbey. He shouldn't have done that—'

'Put her on speaker,' Jimmy instructed her. 'I want to hear what you're saying.'

Charlotte did as she was told.

'You have my assurance that as long as Charlotte is released safely, no more officers will attempt to apprehend you,' Kate said calmly.

'I'm walking out with her now,' Jimmy said. 'One sight of a rifle, if any coppers come near this area, she gets it.'

'A farmer is working to the side of you,' Kate continued. 'He is not - I repeat - he is not one of my team. He is a civilian and does not know what is going on here. I need you to acknowledge that.'

'I hear you,' Jimmy shouted, wrapping his arm around Charlotte's neck once again.

'Now walk, nice and steady, and no sudden moves, okay?'

Charlotte tensed as his arm moved across her neck, and Jimmy tightened his grip. She could smell the oil on his hands once again. The screwdriver was angled towards her face.

'We're coming out now,' Charlotte said, giving a commentary for Kate's benefit. 'I'm not hurt, and I don't believe that I'm in any danger—'

Her voice was steady and in control; she truly believed that Jimmy had no intention of harming her at that moment. He'd given her his message, and she would deliver it. He was fixated on his six o'clock live stream. What would happen after that was anybody's guess.

They stepped out of the doorway and into the open field. The sea was beginning to come in fast now, and the tidal water which surrounded Plover Scar lighthouse was pooling. She could see movement on the beach, but it was far off. There was no chance of Jimmy being tackled by the officers.

They walked slowly around the edge of the abbey, Jimmy alert and tense.

'Is that the farmer?' he asked, looking over toward the edge of the field where the quad bike was parked.

'Yes, he's not one of them, I swear,' Charlotte reassured him.

'We're walking over to the Land Rover now,' Charlotte said, for Kate's benefit.

'Just stay calm,' Kate said. 'We've stood down here, Jimmy. You carry on and make sure Charlotte stays safe—'

The wind was blowing across the speaker, it was difficult to hear her.

The Land Rover was parked so that its rear was facing the abandoned farmhouse. As far as Charlotte could tell, that made life easier for Jimmy because he could get in without directly facing the armed officers. She wondered if the threat of harm from the screwdriver was sufficient grounds for them to shoot him. She felt suddenly vulnerable, wondering if their sights were trained on them at that moment. Jimmy was taller than her. If they shot, it would have to be a headshot. She felt nauseous, bracing herself for what that might mean for her.

'Let's just do this nice and steady, Jimmy,' she whispered to him. 'Kate is as good as her word, you can trust her.'

'I want you in the Land Rover,' he said, abruptly.

'I have to get out of here safe,' Charlotte reminded him. 'You heard what Kate said—'

'You'll be safe, I just have to make sure I'm getting out of here, too.'

'Did you hear that, Kate?' Charlotte began. 'He's taking me in the Land Rover, but he'll let me out.'

'Okay, I hear you,' Kate confirmed. 'But you dare harm her, Jimmy, and we'll come for you. Keep your end of the deal.'

'He will, Kate. He will. He wants to make that broadcast tonight. And, remember Casey and Milo, they're caught up in this too—'

'Stop talking,' Jimmy commanded. 'End the phone connection. You're on your own now.'

He tightened his arm around Charlotte's neck and pushed her against the vehicle.

THIRTY-TWO

'We're going silent, Kate. Everything is alright here.'

Charlotte terminated the open phone line.

'You're hurting me,' she protested.

'Boo hoo,' Jimmy mocked, but he eased off a little.

'You're going to climb up on the driver's side and start the engine when I hand you the keys. Okay?'

He took the keys out of his pocket, and she held out her hand to receive them.

'Not yet,' he snapped. 'When I'm in the vehicle, too. I want you to move the vehicle over toward that farmer—'

'You're not going to hurt him, are you?'

'No, but I'm taking his quad bike. You pull the Land Rover directly in front of him, so the cops don't have a line of sight. Understand? I'll get out, and you can be on your way. You count to fifty, then you're clear to come out. That's how this will work. Got it?'

'Yes, yes, I understand.'

Jimmy pushed Charlotte up into the driver's side, then closed the door on her and locked it with the key.

'Now, open the passenger side,' he called through the glass.

He ran around the back of the vehicle and climbed up to her side. He leaned over and held the screwdriver tip against her neck.

'You're almost out of here,' he said, 'Don't do anything stupid now. Pull up the vehicle at the farmer's side, just like I said, and you'll be out of here in five minutes.'

Charlotte started the engine. It was an old Land Rover, there was little in the way of comfort or style. The diesel engine fired up, and the entire vehicle rattled. The gear stick was reluctant, but she managed to engage it after some effort. The clutch was like nothing she'd handled before, and the vehicle lurched and spluttered forward, stalling.

'Damn, I'm sorry, I've never driven one of these,' she apologised.

'It's just a regular fucking pickup,' Jimmy cursed at her. 'Bloody women drivers, you can only cope with the school run.'

Charlotte felt a prickle run across the length of her body. She tensed momentarily and an uncompromising response was on the tip of her tongue. She imagined Will and Kate cautioning her. She kept her mouth shut. She'd show this arsehole. Charlotte restarted the engine and assertively engaged the gearstick. This time she was more confident on the fierce clutch, and the car moved steadily forward. She drove to the side of the farmer as she'd been instructed.

Hearing a vehicle approaching, the farmer looked up. He was trying to figure out what was going on. Charlotte hoped the stonemason signage would discourage him from doing anything stupid.

'Stop the vehicle, and give me the key,' Jimmy said,

releasing his grip around her neck. 'Now stay here, and count to fifty. Do not move until you've done that.'

She handed him the keys, and he stepped out of the vehicle.

'Give me the fucking key!' she heard Jimmy shout.

'Steady on, mate—'

The farmer protested as she'd expected him to do. She heard a thud, and, just at the side of the passenger side window, she saw a body fall to the ground. She craned her neck to see better. Jimmy threw the Land Rover keys at the farmer who was struggling to pick himself off the ground. Charlotte had already been on the receiving end of one of Jimmy's thumps; the man knew how to land a blow.

She heard the quad bike being started. Charlotte dialled Kate on speed dial, and she picked up straight away.

'What's happening, Charlotte? We've lost sight of him—'

Kate's voice came through the earpiece.

'I'm fine. The farmer's hurt. He's taking the farmer's quad bike—'

She heard revving from beyond the vehicle.

'Shit, we'll lose him. We can't chase him on that thing—'

'Yes, we can,' Charlotte replied. 'Tell your guys not to shoot—'

'Hang on, Charlotte, what are you doing?'

Charlotte tried the driver's door, but being an old vehicle, it was jammed from the inside. She shuffled across to the passenger side, dropped out onto the grass and rushed toward the farmer. He had a bloody nose and seemed dazed.

Jimmy Rylands was heading across the field at some speed toward the narrow footpath and the beach.

'The bugger's making a run for it,' she said to herself as

much as to Kate. She watched as Jimmy hurtled the vehicle directly toward the officer who'd come into the abbey. Jimmy drove straight at him, sending the officer flying in the air.

'Don't worry, help is on the way,' Charlotte reassured the farmer as she picked up the Land Rover keys and rushed around the vehicle to the driver's side. She unlocked the door, climbed back up to the driver's seat and started the engine.

'Don't do this,' Kate pleaded down the phone.

'You're going to lose him if I don't,' Charlotte replied. 'Just make sure your guys are ready when I need them—'

'Charlotte, no, he's dangerous—'

'So am I when someone makes a joke about women drivers,' she replied. She forced the gearstick into first, revved the engine and leaned over to pull the driver's door shut. The clutch bit, and the Land Rover lurched forward. She just missed grasping the door handle. The farmer dodged out of the way as she made a tight turn by the fencing, and she pointed the vehicle at the beach. Both doors were open, but she didn't have time to sort that out. Jimmy had a lead on her, and there was no way the police vehicles could follow him. As far as she knew, Land Rovers were all-terrain, so it was probably the best thing to chase him with.

Charlotte moved through the gears, leaving it in third so she could retain full control as the Land Rover rattled over the grass. She narrowly missed one of the stone ruins around the abbey. She laughed to herself as she thought of the outrage of the local historians cursing the middle-aged woman who'd ploughed into an ancient monument in a stolen truck.

Kate's voice was in her ear all the time. She was getting

radio updates from her officers who could see what was going on from the beach.

'I want you to stop the vehicle, Charlotte. You've just been badly hurt for heaven's sake, you can't go doing stuff like this—'

'I'm fine, Kate, now let me drive. If you're going to nag me like you're my mother, I'm ending the call.'

Kate was silent for a few moments, then she spoke again.

'Okay, Charlotte, have it your way. I can't condone this, you know I can't. But seeing as this isn't being transmitted over the police radios, go and get the bastard—'

Charlotte gasped as the Land Rover dropped from the edge of the field onto the beach and the shingle.

'Jesus Christ—' she cursed, as the entire structure shook and vibrated. She reached for her seatbelt, which was of the old school variety, so required some coaxing. She gave up with it after two tries. The shingle was so difficult to drive on, she needed both hands on the wheel. The open doors on either side of her smashed and crashed as the Land Rover moved from side to side, crunching its way over the stones and sea debris.

'I take it that's not the official view of Morecambe Police?' Charlotte asked.

'You might say that,' came Kate's voice.

'Poor old Herbert might need a new vehicle after this,' Charlotte shouted over the engine roar. 'I hope your budget will stretch to it—'

The wind was taken out of her as she rammed a massive clump of marsh grass. The Land Rover stalled and came to an abrupt stop.

'Fuck,' she cursed, struggling to find her breath. It hurt. She looked along the beach at Jimmy. He was having no such problems on the quad bike which shot across the muddy flats with apparent ease. She knew what he was planning, it was the only way he was getting out of there. He'd move along the beach, away from the police, and resurface along some country lane where he'd be able to avoid capture. She had to track him and see where he left the beach. Otherwise, Kate's team would lose him.

She started up the engine again. The stretch ahead was largely clear of shingle. It was a mix of muddy flats and clumps of marsh grass, with puddled areas forming all around where the tide was beginning to work its way in. She knew it was hazardous, but she had police officers right behind her; it wasn't as if she was acting alone.

She reversed the Land Rover off the clump and headed for the mudflats, the doors on either side swinging as she veered closer to the sea. She would be able to maintain some speed there, it was just mud and puddles. She couldn't risk hitting one of the grass clumps again.

Plover Scar lighthouse was up ahead, she could smell the saltwater as she raced through massive puddles and torrents of seawater swept up at either side of her. The windscreen was becoming plastered in mud, and it was getting difficult to see. Jimmy's brake lights flashed ahead. She had an open path right to him, and she was able to drive faster through the pooled water because her vehicle was heavier. Each time Jimmy hit the water, he'd have to slow, she assumed because he was in danger of flipping the quad bike.

She was almost on his tail now. They'd passed the lighthouse on her left-hand side, and he was within easy reach. She floored the accelerator and crunched the gears into fourth. As she did so, she veered the Land Rover to the right, intending to circle in front of Jimmy and force him to stop. Instead, she veered too far, crashing at speed through a massive pool of tidal water that had woven its way through the flats. She felt the truck plane through the water and fought to steady the steering wheel. Hidden within the pool was a mound of mud. The driver's side raced up the rise, and she sensed it flipping as she hurtled out of control across the beach. She felt the balance change the moment the vehicle tipped on the sandbank; it was turning over. The door to her side was wide open. She took her hands off the wheel and launched herself out of the side of the Land Rover as it crashed on its side and sent a massive wave of seawater crashing along the beach.

She landed on a patch of sodden mud and rolled a few times before coming to a stop. She lifted her head to see Jimmy Rylands riding off into the distance. She braced herself to stand up. As she tensed her legs, she felt herself sinking into the mud. Every time she wriggled, her legs sunk deeper in. All around her the water was lapping as the sea continued to make its way inland.

'Kate?' she said, wondering if the phone line was still open. There was no reply. She was out there alone, and she was stuck.

THIRTY-THREE

Morecambe, 1996

Amanda Pickering had something on her mind that morning. During the daily briefing, she would smile at Frank and nod at him, barely paying attention to what was being said. The moment they were dismissed, she made her way over to him.

'So, have you heard the good news?' she asked.

'No, but you're looking very pleased with yourself,' he replied.

'Just call me Detective Constable,' she beamed at him.

'Never? Really? How? Who told you?'

'Check your memos. It was in my pigeonhole this morning. I hear through the grapevine that you got your transfer approved, too. We're going to be detectives, Frank.'

Frank felt his heart beating faster. At last, this is what he wanted. It would work better with the kids. It had been some time coming.

'Will you join me for a celebratory drink after work?'

Frank liked Amanda. He knew she liked him, she'd

made that clear enough. But he'd never thought of her that way until well after Evie died. Now, perhaps, here was the chance of a fresh start. It would be good for the kids to have a woman around the house, too, particularly for Kate. She was at such a difficult age, he always felt like he was failing as her father.

'Do you know what, Amanda, I think I will. Can we meet after I've been home though? I like to see the kids after school and check in on them first. Is that okay?'

'Frank, any teenager would be proud to call you their dad. Besides, I'd like to see my two before we go out as well. They've both been a bit difficult since the divorce. I like to show my face now and then, just to make sure they don't end up as our clients in the police cells.'

Frank laughed.

'Eight o'clock, then? How about The Smuggler's Den in Poulton-le-Sands? They have a nice open fire there.'

'You're on! See you there.'

PC Pickering headed off to the locker room, Frank checked his pigeonhole. There it was, just like Amanda had said. A memo from the brass, confirming his transfer to Detective Constable. At last, he'd made detective.

'Hey, Larry, have you got a minute?' he called over as he spotted his friend about to leave the briefing room.

'Morning, Frank, how does it feel to be all on your own again?'

'It's only for a day, Larry. What time does your training start?'

'Fifteen minutes. I was just going to grab a coffee. What have they got you on today?'

'I'm on a town centre beat, nothing too arduous. I wanted to have a word before you find it out on the grapevine—'

'What, you and Amanda Pickering have a thing for each other?'

'Come on, Larry, we've talked about this before. But I am seeing her tonight. We've got something to celebrate—'

'You've got a child on the way?'

'Stop teasing, you miserable bastard. They're making us both detectives.'

Larry shook Frank's hand firmly.

'Congratulations, mate. I mean it. I'll be sad to see you go, but I know it's what you want. Detective Constable Frank Allan. It has a nice ring to it. When do you start?'

'Monday,' Frank replied, pleased that Larry was taking it so well.

'That's fast. Still, it'll be good for you and the kids. Well done, that's a great result.'

'While you're here, did you manage to follow up with Jonny Irving over that motorcycle chase?' Frank checked. 'I've been meaning to do it for days, but I keep getting called off to domestic incidents and burglaries.'

'No, I haven't, sorry. Is that drunk prick still bothering you? You've got your own kids to worry about, Frank. Jonny Irving's kids and that girl you're so worried about will have to take care of themselves.'

'That's where you and I differ,' Frank replied. 'Besides, I'm sure something is up with those kids. There's something they're not telling me.'

Larry congratulated Frank once again and was on his way. Frank sorted himself out in the locker room and headed out on his beat. As he walked along the Morecambe streets, he savoured the experience, knowing that he'd miss this contact with the public once he started as a detective. Being a beat copper was all he knew. But the time was right, this was good for the family.

After making a couple of routine calls, Frank decided that it was time to check in on Jonny Irving. He'd promised the Gogarty girl that he would, and all the time he hadn't done it, he felt he was letting her down.

He braced himself as he walked up the driveway to Irving's house. The pubs weren't open yet, so that increased the chances of Jonny being home, at least.

He knocked at the door. He hoped the kids weren't at home, he could speak more freely if they were out of the house. It was his lucky day; not only had he had his transfer confirmed, but Jonny Irving was in, too. He could resolve this final, outstanding matter before making the move to detective.

Jonny answered the door in a pair of bright blue Y-fronts and a crumpled vest. Frank thought back to the woman he'd seen Jonny with at the ATC event. He seemed to have two personalities.

'Ah fuck, a'hoped it'd be Jehovah's Witnesses at th'door,' he scowled, 'not th'fucking cops.'

'Nice to see you too, Jonny. Can I come in? You must be cold like that'

'Naw, yer can stay on th'step.'

'I want to talk to you about an incident at Heysham Moss in which a young girl was being harassed by a motor-cycle rider—'

Frank paused to see if Jonny gave anything away. He didn't even flinch.

'Was that you, Jonny?'

'Fuck off! I don't even have a bike, yer bastard!'

'So, who was it, Jonny?'

'Fuck knows, you're th'copper around here.'

Frank could see this was going nowhere quickly.

'Look, Jonny, I know it was you, but I can't prove it. If I

see or hear you troubling young girls, I'll be on you like a tonne of bricks. Understood?'

'Fuck off, it wasn't me—'

'I mean it, Jonny. Consider this a final warning. Besides, didn't I see you with a new girlfriend in town the other day?'

If Jonny had kept a straight face when Frank mentioned the incident with Casey, his expression gave the game away this time.

'Yer can't go sayin' stuff like that, w'yer accusations and stuff. I'll lose my fucking benefits if yer go round sayin' things like that. Fuck off, we're done here!'

Jonny slammed the door in Frank's face. It was not the interaction Frank was hoping for, but at least Jonny knew he was being watched. It looked to Frank like there might be some benefit fraud going on, too. He'd keep that to himself, exposing that could only hurt Jonny's kids.

The rest of the day passed without mishap, and Frank was looking forward to his drink with PC Pickering by the time he'd got home, changed and had some food with the kids. He checked in the hallway mirror that he was looking presentable, then shouted up the stairs.

'I'm going out for my drink, kids. See you later!'

'Okay Dad,' came Kate's voice. Brett probably had head-phones on.

'By the way, I'm a detective now!' he shouted.

'Nice one, Dad,' Kate replied. 'Have a good night out.'

Frank shrugged. He'd tell them about it properly the next day. He wished he'd said at the evening meal, but Brett had been excited about something at school, and he'd got distracted. There was plenty of time to talk the next day.

As Frank rested his hand on the front door handle, the telephone in the hallway started to ring.

'I'll get it!' Frank called up the stairs.

'Hello.'

'PC Allan?'

'Yes. Who's speaking?'

'It's Casey Gogarty. I need your help. I'm really scared. I think he's going to hurt me—'

THIRTY-FOUR

Charlotte looked around, taking in the entire beach, trying to figure out how far she'd come. Kate's team would be following her, she knew that much, but would they even see her out there in the middle of what was a huge expanse of mud, sand, shingle, and marsh grass? Every time she wriggled, she sank deeper into the cold, wet mud.

She'd barely had time to think about her previous wounds. Her chest was still tight and sore, and it didn't help to have her legs restricted by the mud. Any attempt she made to twist or pull herself out resulted in straining the upper part of her body. She would have to wait for help to arrive.

The gentle sloshing of the water all around her was unnerving. The sea was coming in, but not like a beach, where its approach would be even and predictable. The water from the bay was more predatory, filling channels and pools, circling her with stealth, waiting for its opportunity to consume her.

Charlotte forced herself to stay calm. She'd been in

worse situations; at least the policing team knew she was out there. So, where the hell were they?

She raised her body so she could use the lighthouse to estimate how far she'd driven up the coastline. She was surprised to see how far off it was; she'd been driving faster than she'd thought.

Charlotte had never experienced anything like this mud trap before. She felt ridiculous, like a child getting a welly boot stuck in a muddy puddle. But it was for real. Every move she made sucked her in deeper. She'd seen the movies; all she had to do was lie flat and still and wait for help to arrive. And, to hope that the tide wasn't in any rush to come in.

She wondered where her mobile phone was. She still couldn't quite believe that she'd leapt from the Land Rover like that. But faced with the prospect of it rolling on its side and crashing her across the width of a vehicle that offered very little in the way of padding, she had made the split-second decision to leap out. Looking at the upturned vehicle across the mudflat confirmed that had probably been the best decision. At least she'd had a soft landing; she reckoned she'd be contending with physical injuries, too, if she'd still been stuck in Herbert's truck.

Between the lapping waves, she caught the sound of a steady beep to her side. She moved slowly, not wanting to sink any further, and saw the Bluetooth earpiece sitting at her side. It was muddy but appeared to be working. She pressed the small button on the tiny unit, wiped it on her top and inserted it in her ear.

'Charlotte?'

'Yes - Kate?'

'Where are you? Are you okay? My guys are heading up

the beach. They reported a sighting of the Land Rover flipped over on the mud—'

Charlotte's eye was drawn by the illuminated screen of her mobile phone which had become lodged in the mud a couple of metres ahead of her when she had jumped out of the Land Rover. It didn't matter that it was out of reach, the Bluetooth was in range, somebody would be able to rescue her now.

'I'm fine, I jumped clear. Did he get away?'

'Yes, he got away. He must have had another motorcycle parked along the road. Two of our officers found the quad bike abandoned up a country lane. Whatever he's riding, it wasn't the same bike as last time. He probably drove straight by us.'

'Damn. I'm in a bit of trouble here, Kate. I think I can see your officers now. Can you raise them on the radio?'

'Yes, are you injured?'

'No, I'm sinking in the mud. I can't move. The tidal water is getting uncomfortably close, too. I'm not up to my neck or anything like that. But I'm not sure how long I have until the water reaches me—'

'I'm calling the RNLI on a separate phone. Leave this line open, Charlotte. I'll tell the team to look out for you. Can you wave at them?'

'If I do, I'll be up to my neck in mud when they arrive. Tell them to keep heading for the Land Rover, they'll see me from there.'

'Stay on the line—'

Charlotte began reminding Kate that she wasn't intending on going anywhere, but she was away already. She could hear Kate alerting the coastguard and updating the officers of her approximate whereabouts via the radio.

'Okay, I'm back. They're sending out the hovercraft from Morecambe. They won't be long. You've also got three officers heading your way. You certainly know how to make a splash, Charlotte - no pun intended.'

'He wants safe passage to Spain—' Charlotte began, suddenly remembering why she'd spoken to Rylands in the first place.

'He knows he won't get it, surely?' Kate replied.

'He wants to find his mother and share his big revelation with her, I think. Do you know where she is yet?'

'No. Cross-channel cooperation has become a little more difficult of late. It'll take some time.'

Charlotte felt a splash of water soak her feet. The sea was circling behind her, drawing in closer all the time. Her instinct was to move away, but as she did, she felt the mud suck her in a little deeper. If she kept talking to Kate, it would keep her mind off what was happening all around her. Charlotte knew it would make the rescue operation more hazardous if she panicked. She had to remain calm.

'Will you make him an offer?' she asked. 'Or, will you try and find him?'

'We tried locating him via mobile phone masts, but it pretty well tells us what we know already. He's in Morecambe. We can't pin him down close enough, so that's no use. It's a waiting game. We'll tell him that we're seeking the permissions to allow him to exit the country and string him along. In the meantime, we have to hope he gives his location away.'

Charlotte heard shouting up ahead. The three officers had reached the Land Rover and were calling out to her.

'One moment, Kate,' Charlotte said, looking up to see how close they were.

'I'm over here,' she shouted. 'It's dangerous, don't come too close.'

'Are you injured?' came a male voice.

'My dignity is, but there are no physical injuries that I can see.'

Two of the officers attempted to move closer to her. They got as far as her phone, then backed off.

'It's too muddy,' one of them called over. 'The RNLI guys are on their way. I'll take your phone—'

'Careful—' Charlotte began. He'd cut off the call with Kate. She reared up to yell at him to leave it where it was, but felt herself sink a little deeper as she did so. She gave up and stayed motionless in the mud. The water was becoming more confident now, that's all she could hear all around her. She rested a moment, figuring she'd need to conserve her energy for the forthcoming rescue.

At last, she heard a motor in the distance. This had to be them. She raised her head and searched the beach. There it was, the distinctive orange craft, shooting across the water and mud with no difficulty whatsoever. It made a wide circuit around her and came to a stop on the mud.

'Charlotte Grayson?' one of the team members shouted. They were fully equipped with helmets, life jackets, and all-weather suits; she knew she was now in good hands.

'Yes, that's me. It's very muddy around here, be careful—'

She saw the man chuckling at her words. She was teaching her granny to suck eggs.

The RNLI team worked with incredible efficiency. They assembled mud boards to her side and in front of her. One of the team dragged over a plastic cradle which appeared to Charlotte like an adult size sledge. One of the RNLI team stretched out across a mud board and began to assess her situation. As he started speaking to her confidently and calmly, Charlotte thanked karma that she always donated to the RNLI whenever she got the opportunity. She was getting her money's worth, that was for sure.

'Are you in any pain or discomfort? Are you injured? Is anybody else out here with you?'

He ran through the various permutations whilst examining the mud around her, checking her legs, and making sure she hadn't gone into shock.

'This would have been a lot worse in winter,' he reassured her, 'That water can be icy cold. You seem okay. We're going to get you out of here now.'

Charlotte could have kissed him. He began to dig around her legs. Now and then, he'd stop and check she was alright. One of the team members was taking photographs.

'Can I get copies of those?' she asked. 'I work on the local paper. I'd love to write a story on this.'

'No problem,' the man replied. 'I'll take plenty of extras, so you have lots to select from. I'll make sure I get your good side.'

The distraction had been good. It had relaxed her, and her legs were now free.

'Okay, I want you to move over to the mud board, and I'm going to pull you at the same time. Work with me, but try not to kick your legs, or you'll sink again. Ready?'

The man pulled her, and she worked with him, allowing her legs to stay motionless. There was a slurping sound as her left foot squelched out of the mud, then she felt her body suddenly supported by the mud board. She was out. Thank God.

'Thank you,' she said, 'Thank you so much.'

She sat up and looked around her. It had been difficult to get a feel for how far the tide had come in whilst she was laid out, prostrate on the mud. What she saw shocked her. If they hadn't come so fast, she'd have been fighting to keep her head out of the water within minutes. Next time somebody collecting for the RNLI shook a charity box in front of her, they'd be getting an extra generous donation.

THIRTY-FIVE

By the time Kate arrived, Charlotte was being attended to by a medical team that had driven out from the local surgery to assist with the rescue. They arrived in a 4-wheel drive which was suitable for navigating along the closest lane to the stretch of the beach where all the action was taking place.

'You appear to be fine,' the doctor said. 'Only, your heart seems to be racing faster than it would be normally. Do you have a heart condition?'

Charlotte felt fine, and she didn't want to draw attention to Henderson's off-the-books medical services.

'I think it's just the excitement of it all,' Charlotte replied. 'I'm desperate to get out of these clothes, but I'm good, honestly—'

'Here she is, the Lara Croft of Morecambe Bay.'

It felt immediately reassuring to hear Kate's voice again.

'You'd have been proud of the way I leapt out of that Land Rover,' Charlotte smiled. She pulled the quick-warming blanket around her. Her wet clothes were what was making her feel cold, rather than the weather. Over on the beach, a pulley truck was salvaging Herbert's vehicle which had already been pushed back onto its four wheels. Tyre boards were being used to stabilise it on the mud, but it was a battle with the tide, which was almost at engine level.

'Any word on Herbert?' Charlotte asked. 'Please tell me he's okay.'

'He is,' Kate reassured her. 'Just shaken and a bit shocked by it all. A couple of constables found him at his house. He doesn't live that far from here. Rylands must have found his details via the livery on his truck. Anyway, he tied him up this morning and stole the vehicle. He left a motorcycle up one of the country lanes so he could make his escape. He's a canny one, that's for certain.'

'I think you're right about the big finale,' Charlotte said. 'I'm beginning to wonder if he even cares about being caught. It's like he has some kind of death wish. He's all but given up creeping around now. It takes some bravado to do what he just did—'

'Er, you know you could be describing yourself there. Do you not see what just happened here? I sometimes wonder if you have a death wish, the way you behave.'

Herbert's car was now clear of the mud and being towed onto the shingle.

'I hope I haven't wrecked his Land Rover,' Charlotte began. 'I still need to sort out an arrangement with the two damaged e-scooters. It's getting a bit expensive. I'll have to check that scrap yard we went to and see if I can find an old Land Rover to offer Herbert.'

'Let's get you home,' Kate suggested. 'I take it she's clear for take-off, Doctor?'

The medic was packing up his bag and making signals that it was time to move back to his car.

'She's good to go. Maybe just get your regular GP to check your heart if you can?'

'Will do,' Charlotte smiled. She had no intention of checking in with her GP. A little abnormal heart activity was to be expected after the week she'd just had. Besides, she felt fine.

'I'll get an officer to run you home.' Kate offered. 'I suggest you have a nice, long shower and watch afternoon TV. You deserve it after that.'

'What's the time now?' Charlotte asked. 'Are you planning anything for Jimmy's six o'clock live stream?'

'It's just past two o'clock now,' Kate replied, checking her phone. 'Oh, by the way, here's your phone. It's a bit muddy, but it's still showing signs of life.'

Charlotte took the phone from Kate. She was so pleased she'd opted for a waterproof model that day in Lancaster after her jet-ski chase with Vinnie Mace wrecked her last one. It was coping well with her lifestyle.

Kate helped her up to her feet and hugged her.

'Be careful, Charlotte, please don't hurt yourself.'

Charlotte squeezed in tight, then immediately recoiled as a sharp pain ripped through her chest.

'Ouch! That's the bruising from my near-death experience. Sorry, it's nothing personal.'

A uniformed officer escorted Charlotte to a police car, and he opened the passenger side door for her. He'd placed that day's newspaper on the seat to protect it from the mud that was caked all over her clothing.

'I feel like a misbehaving dog,' she smiled as she climbed in.

The officer accompanied her to the front door of the guest house.

'Do you want me to come in?' he asked.

'No, I'm fine, honestly. My family is home. I just need to get out of these clothes and have a good shower.'

Downstairs was empty, so Charlotte headed directly for the stairs. As she reached the final step at the top, she could hear the hum of Will and Lucia's voices in the family accommodation.

'What the hell?' Will said as she stepped into the kitchen. 'You look like a swamp monster. Are you alright?'

'What happened, Mum?' Lucia asked. Charlotte could see she'd been crying. She reckoned her daughter was probably going out of her mind after Milo's earlier disappearance.

'Remember that song we used to sing about Doctor Foster going to Gloucester?' Charlotte asked.

Lucia seemed confused.

'Yes.'

'Well, I fell in a puddle right up to my middle.'

The bell from the reception area rang.

'You'd best get that,' Charlotte suggested. 'I don't think I'm in a fit state to deal with enquiries at the moment.'

'I'll see to it,' Will offered, getting up from his chair. 'You get yourself showered and changed.'

Charlotte kissed Lucia on her head, then made for the bathroom. She peeled off her clothes and ran the shower hot. She stayed under the water for ten minutes before starting to wash her hair. The water felt glorious after the cold, salty mud of the bay.

After some time, she was ready to step out. She wrapped a towel around her hair, dried herself off, pulled the towel around herself for modesty purposes, and walked across the landing to the bedroom. There she threw on a pair of jogging pants and a comfortable top. She felt immediately renewed, if a little stiff still.

Will came into the bedroom.

'I take it your adventure with Kate got out of hand?' he asked.

'You might say that,' she replied, expecting him to give her a hard time.

'Look, I can see you're fine, and I know you're just trying to help. Lucia has been going out of her mind all day over Milo. I'm not here to hassle you. I just wanted you to know that someone is waiting for you downstairs. Are you up to seeing them, or shall I send him packing? He didn't want to give me a name. He said you'll want to speak to him, though.'

'It's fine, I'll see him now,' Charlotte replied, intrigued by who was waiting for her downstairs.

She finished towelling her hair and ran her fingers through it swiftly to give it some kind of shape and tidiness. She then rushed down the stairs to the reception area. A man was sitting there, and he looked up as soon as he heard her making her way down the stairs. It was Seth Irving.

THIRTY-SIX

Morecambe, 1996

'Where are you, Casey?'

'I'm at my Nan's caravan at Cockerham Sands—'

'Are you safe at the moment?'

'I'm calling from the payphone at the campsite. I don't have much money left. Once this coin gets swallowed up, I'm out of cash.'

'How did you get there?'

'On my motorcycle. He came to the house. Mum and Dad are away at the moment with my Nan. I stayed at home to revise for my exams—'

'Slow down, Casey. Can you see him now?'

Frank's mind was racing. He should have written this up in his notebook. There was no record of his interactions with Jonny because he'd been convinced the problem would go away. And now, here he was, a newly appointed detective, and he'd messed this up. In that moment of decision, Frank resolved to finish this once and for all. He'd catch

Jonny in the act and process him at the station. He couldn't let this one slip any longer.

'He's riding around the campsite asking people if they know where I am. It's not like I'm easy to miss with these glasses on, is it?'

Frank said nothing. But, Casey was right. Whenever witnesses were being questioned, they always noticed the big stuff: unusual hairstyles, distinctive clothing, unfamiliar accents and, of course, spectacles that stood out because of their thick lenses. If Frank was a crook, he'd have worn a distinctive cap and T-shirt, maybe one with a slogan on it, bought some cheap sunglasses from one of the shops along the promenade, and nobody would ever pick him out in a line-up. Witnesses always missed the crucial minutiae.

'Is there somewhere you can go, where he won't find you? I'll come and pick you up, take you somewhere safe and sort out Jonny. How does that sound?'

'I can hide by the old abbey. He won't look for me there. Do you know where it is? It's along the footpath as you reach the beach—'

'I know roughly where you are. It's getting dark. Will you be alright out there?'

'I can't stay here. I've just seen somebody point over to my Nan's caravan. He'll find my motorcycle there. He'll know I'm around here somewhere—'

The phone pips sounded. They had a couple of seconds to sign off.

'Go to the abbey, I'm on my way,' Frank urged her. 'Stay safe, and keep out of sight.'

The phone clicked dead. Lots of people were buying mobile phones, but they were still too expensive for Frank's tastes. He wished he'd had one right at that moment. He put the phone receiver back in its cradle, then picked it up again straight away. He flicked through the phone book and found Amanda's number. She used her maiden name at work to avoid complications with the criminal fraternity. Most cops didn't bother with the phone book, but Amanda's husband was listed under the marital surname. Frank dialled her number, hoping that she hadn't set off early. One of her children answered.

'Hello?'

'Hi, it's Frank Allan here. Is your mum still there?'

'Mummmmm! She's coming.'

The child at the other end of the line placed the receiver at the side of the phone. There was thumping down the line, the sound of Amanda coming down the stairs, Frank reckoned.

'Amanda, it's Frank. Something important has come up. I'm going to have to cry off tonight. I'm so sorry.'

'Is something wrong with the kids?' Amanda asked, parental concern in her voice.

'No, not my kids. Do you remember the children I told you about the other day? Something just came up with one of them. Consider it a welfare matter.'

'You're a dedicated beat constable right until the bitter end, Frank. No problem, you sort it out. Let's do it tomorrow night then, yes? Same time, same place?'

'You're on,' Frank replied, relieved that she hadn't made it difficult. He ended the call. Kate was at the top of the stairs, hovering.

'Everything alright, dad?'

'Just a change of plan. I'm heading out. I'll be back soon. I love you, Kiddo.'

'Yeah, yeah, love you too, Dad.'

'Tell Brett I love him, too. He never takes those damn headphones off.'

'Ha-ha, will do, Dad. See you later!'

Kate retreated to her bedroom. Frank paused for a moment, wondering if he was doing the right thing. Yes, he'd been stupid not writing up his encounters with Jonny in his notebook. From an official point of view, he'd record this as his first formal encounter with the man. That way his paperwork trail would be right when he moved over to detective duties. Besides, Jonny was a small-time crook, incapable of doing any real harm.

Frank picked up his keys and headed out of the house to the car. It was a wet and wild night, not the best time for Casey to be out on her own. He checked the glove compartment of the car; there was a torch in there for emergencies. Even better, the battery still worked. Frank started up the engine. He'd been careless over Jonny Irving, thinking he could protect the man's children by dealing with him off-the-record. He'd pushed it too far now. Jonny Irving had forced Frank into resolving this issue, once and for all.

THIRTY-SEVEN

'Seth? What the hell—'

'I can't wait around forever, Charlotte. I have to speak to Gogs if she's in town. I won't let her suffer for what happened—'

Things were moving too fast for Charlotte. She was still unsteady on her feet after the rescue on the mudflats.

'Come into the dining room. Take a seat,' she offered. 'I take it you're on Josh's bike?'

Seth nodded.

'It's just outside the front door. You were easy enough to find. This place was here when I was a kid.'

'Why did you leave Josh's lodge? You know it puts you in danger, don't you?'

'Listen, Charlotte. I've been locked up in prison for twenty-five years. Just picture that. You'd have been - what - in your thirties? Can you imagine that length of time being locked away?'

Charlotte thought about it. Lucia and Olli hadn't reached that age yet. It was an eternity to be denied your freedom.

'When I was a kid, I took legal advice to plead guilty to Brewer's murder. I was promised I'd be out in no time because of my age. But that didn't happen, did it? That bloody newspaper got the bit between its teeth and challenged every parole board hearing I ever had through a team of lawyers representing Brewer's wife. Do you know what it feels like to think they threw the key away?'

Charlotte shook her head. It didn't even bear thinking about.

'I took the full force of everybody's hatred, just because I happened to be eighteen when I went to court. It's like they couldn't get their hands on the others, so they went for me—'

He paused a moment and rubbed his eyes.

'I didn't mind taking the hit for the other kids, we agreed that, but I never expected to be in prison for twenty-five years. And, all because it suits a national newspaper to turn me into some child-killer monster.'

'Did you kill David Brewer?' Charlotte asked.

'Would you believe me if I said I didn't?'

'I think I might, actually.'

They sat in silence for a few moments.

'It was complicated, what happened. We were kids, remember that. And, we were very scared—'

'I've heard about your dad,' Charlotte interrupted. 'What was he like?'

'He was the monster,' Seth replied. 'It would have been worth going to prison, just for a short time, to get away from him. I hated him—'

'Is he dead?' Charlotte asked. 'He just disappeared. Nobody seemed to care very much.'

Seth's face coloured.

'Nobody gave a shit that he went missing. It was the

habit of a lifetime for him. He was flaky all through our childhood, coming and going. He resented us, I think.'

'Was David Brewer a paedophile?'

Charlotte couldn't believe her luck that she had Seth to herself. And, he was talking, too. Without all the police formalities, he was happy to answer her questions.

'No, Brewer was no paedophile. It was just a crazy thing that somebody overheard that got out of hand. It's funny, I've had years to think about all of this. Now I'm an adult, I see lots of things more clearly—'

'Go on,' Charlotte urged.

'Brewer was just a deeply unhappy man. He hated teaching, but he was caught in it. Just like I had bars keeping me in jail, he had his job imprisoning him. And, he hated it. He wanted to be in the forces. Did you know he had fits?'

'Yes, I'd heard that. Epilepsy. Did he suffer badly with it?'

'Yes, enough to screw up his career choices. He was like a different man at ATC. It was what he wanted to do. At school, I think he was just deeply unhappy. And, you know his mate in the PE department was screwing his wife?'

Charlotte nodded. She'd been trapped by teaching herself. It wasn't like normal office jobs; you couldn't just shuffle papers at your desk all day and hide away. Every day, you had to confront the kids in the classroom. If it wasn't what you wanted to do, it was hell on earth, she knew that. She also knew how difficult it was to walk away when you needed to bring in an income.

'Did Brewer know?' she asked. She was beginning to form a different view of the man.

'We were only kids, remember, I just saw them snogging once at an ATC event we had. I saw Brewer watching them from across the parade ground. They thought they couldn't be seen, but I saw them, and so did he. I think it just made him feel more trapped. The only time I ever saw any joy in his face was at ATC. He was like Jekyll and Hyde.'

'Where did the paedophile accusation come from?'

'It was ridiculous. Gogs thought it was originated from a time when she fell out with Brewer in the Arndale Centre. They were sitting on some seats. Brewer was trying to help her. Other people were sitting close by. Gogs said she got upset with him and threatened to tell people he was a paedophile if he didn't back off. She told me she apologised to him later, but the damage was done. Someone must have heard her. And, a copper came to speak to her immediately after. Gogs wasn't sure, but she reckoned that's when it started. You know what rumours are like. Particularly in a small town like this.'

Charlotte's head was pounding with all the new information. At last, the story was beginning to tie together.

'Casey Gogarty is Gogs, or Goggles, isn't she?' Charlotte asked. 'I think she must be. I found her old spectacles up in her room—'

'She's staying here?' Seth asked. 'Can I see her room?'

Charlotte ran through all the privacy concerns that might have been thrown at her. This man hadn't seen his friend for years and years. It seemed a small thing to ask for. And, with Casey missing, it might, perhaps, provide a clue.

'She is Gogs?'

'Yes,' he nodded, 'we never called her Casey back then. You know what kids are like. Everybody had a nickname.'

'I can take you to her room, but we can't disturb anything. I'd be hauled over the coals if anybody ever found out about it. But, I'd like you to see her spectacles, just to be certain.'

Charlotte stood up and led the way up the stairs. Seth followed, quietly, almost as if he were about to view a dead body. In many ways, it must have seemed to him like reaching out to a ghost.

Charlotte used her pass key to open the door. Seth paused a moment before entering.

'The glasses are in here,' Charlotte explained. He followed her through to the bathroom.

When Seth saw them, he cried.

'Poor Gogs,' he sniffed. 'Those bloody National Health glasses. They were terrible things. Look at the lenses, it's like double-glazing. She was so self-conscious in them. I don't think she ever knew how many of the boys at school fancied her. At least she would have got her contact lenses in the end. It's all she could think about, other than motocross, of course.'

He picked up the glasses and moved them in his hand like they were a precious item from the past.

'I came here because I want to help Casey. I did it all those years back, and I'll do it again—'

'How did you help her?' Charlotte asked. 'Why was she in trouble?'

'My dad, mainly,' Seth answered. 'He wouldn't leave her alone. Brewer and that cop - I heard you mention him at Josh's lodge—'

'Frank Allan? DCI Summers' dad.'

'Yes, that's him. He was a good guy. He didn't deserve what happened to him. He was only trying to help—'

Seth stopped speaking as they exited the bathroom and spotted Josh's book at the side of Casey's bed. Seth picked it up and flicked through the pages. Something fell out and landed face down on the carpet.

'Look at my little brother. I'm so proud of him. Casey

helped him with his writing, you know. If it wasn't for her, I think he'd have given up. Brewer was a right bastard to him over his dyslexia. As I said, he was Jekyll and Hyde.'

Seth bent over to pick up whatever was on the floor. It was a photograph which he studied carefully for a moment. Charlotte was able to get a clear view of it. It was a picture of Casey, on holiday somewhere exotic. She had her arm around a young man, mid-twenties she'd have guessed. They looked happy and comfortable together; he was her son, rather than a partner.

As Seth examined the picture, his shoulders hunched up and a single tear dropped onto the photograph.

'Oh, hell, Gogs. You did it. You got away. I'm so happy for you.'

THIRTY-EIGHT

'He's your son, isn't he?' Charlotte asked.

Seth couldn't speak. He was so taken aback by the image.

'He must be twenty-five years old. He's a good-looking kid.'

Seth swallowed hard.

'I think he's mine. God, how do we even start unravelling all this?'

'Why do you only think he might be yours?'

'I haven't spoken to Gogs since that night. The night Brewer died. We had a moment before I told her to run - a brief moment alone. She told me then. I think that's what she told me. It's why we made the pact. It was made in a hurry. We were protecting Gogs. We were kids. It would be different now.'

He couldn't take his eyes off the photograph. He was fixed to the spot, staring at it, as if it had changed the epicentre of his world.

'I want to find her,' Seth said, resolved and determined

now. 'I want to speak to Gogs before I tell anybody else about this stuff. I have to get things straight in my head.'

'I don't know where she is,' Charlotte replied, gently. 'The police don't know where she is either. This Jimmy Rylands fellow has her. Are you sure you don't know anything more about him?'

'He was just some kid at school. Do you remember all the kids from your school? I don't. I remember he was a bit of a dick. He would hang around the motorbikes when we were out on the grass, always bothering us for a ride. He was just one of the younger kids. I was seventeen then. Me and Gogs took Eric and Robbie out once, but the young ones were too scared as a rule; it was too much trouble.'

Charlotte realised she hadn't got her phone. She'd left it on charge when she had gone for a shower. She'd wiped off the mud and left it to dry on a wad of kitchen towel.

'Can you wait for me in the reception area, Seth? We need to talk about what happens next. I should check that DCI Summers hasn't called.'

'And, Frank Allan was her dad, you say? No wonder she wanted to speak to me at Josh's lodge. I want to speak to her, too. Properly. But, only once I've seen Gogs. There's nothing they can do to touch me now, I've served my time. But I have to make things right with Goggles.'

Charlotte watched Seth slip the photograph into his pocket. She didn't challenge him; she couldn't begrudge him that, after all the years he'd been locked up in prison.

She locked up Casey's room. Seth made his way down the stairs, and Charlotte headed for the family accommodation. Will and Lucia were watching TV. Lucia's eyes were no longer red. They were laughing at some comedy show.

'I'm heading out for a while,' she began.

'Who was that downstairs?' Will asked.

'Oh, just a query for an afternoon event and buffet. Nothing interesting.'

Something amusing happened on the TV screen, and Will and Lucia laughed. Will didn't challenge Charlotte any further. At least Lucia was occupied now. It would save her going quietly crazy while she fretted about Milo.

She picked her phone up from the kitchen. It was showing some signs of moisture behind the screen, but it activated without any problems. It had full charge now; she was good to go.

Charlotte picked up the car keys and shouted goodbye to Will and Lucia. They were so distracted, it was all they could do to acknowledge her. She ran down the stairs, taking two steps at a time, back to Seth who was waiting in the reception area still.

'There's a message on my phone,' she said, as he looked up from the photograph. He'd been studying it again.

'I know that there's nothing left between me and Gogs after all these years. I wouldn't even know how to be around a woman after spending my life cooped up with all those men. But, I have a right to know about my son, don't I? That's fair, isn't it?'

'I think Casey has unfinished business of her own,' Charlotte answered. 'Why else would she be here? I think she's seeking answers, too.'

She redialled the number.

'This is Jimmy Rylands,' she whispered. 'He called me while I was in the shower.'

Seth looked up from the photo and watched her take the call.

'Charlotte?'

She placed him on speakerphone.

'Yes.'

'So, you got away then? Again.'

'Yes, you too. Nice escape. At some time, our luck has to run out.'

'Speak for yourself,' Jimmy taunted. 'So long as I get my live stream, I don't care what happens after that. Did you sort out my request?'

'I asked DCI Summers, and she's running it by the suits. She can't give permission without a nod from her superiors. You understand that, right?'

'She has until six o'clock. I have to know by then. They'll figure out where I am when we go live—'

He paused a moment, thrown off by a sound in the distance. It was a bell, like a phone ringing. Only, he didn't sound like he was in a house.

'Hey, Jimmy, it's Seth Irving—'

Seth shouted across from his chair.

There was silence at the end of the phone. It allowed Charlotte to listen to the sound in the background. She'd figured out where he was hiding. She could barely contain herself.

'Seth? Is that you?'

'It is. You didn't get me, Jimmy. You set fire to a harmless tramp, instead. How does that make you feel?'

Charlotte could almost sense the rage that was making its way down the phone.

'So, you're all returning to the scene of the crime. There's a change of plan, Charlotte. Are you listening? Is that cop with you?'

'I'm listening. DCI Summers isn't here. I'm at the guest house. Where you spray-painted my dining room wall and terrified my daughter, remember?'

'Yeah, sorry about that. But if you'd backed off then, things would have been so much better for you, don't you think?'

'I want to see Gogs,' Seth demanded.

'And, you can,' Jimmy replied. 'I want you here for the live stream.'

'I'm not being part of any crazy plan you're hatching. Just let me see Gogs—'

'I'll call you later. Be ready to come here. I'll call you. I'll tell you where and when. If I tell you now, you'll tell the police. Wait for my call.'

Jimmy terminated the conversation at his end.

'Dammit!' Seth cursed, thumping the arm of the chair.

Charlotte checked the time. It was nearing four o'clock. Two hours until Jimmy revealed whatever it was he wanted to share with the world.

'Come on, we're going,' Charlotte said.

'Where?'

'To find Casey. To sort out Jimmy. He's not armed. You can handle yourself, can't you? You can take on Jimmy Rylands if you have to. I'll take care of Casey if you promise to deal with Jimmy.'

'Yes. I learned how to look after myself in prison. I can handle Jimmy Rylands if I have to. You're sure he's not armed?'

'Only with an oily screwdriver, as far as I know.'

'Okay, I'll take that chance. Only, we don't know where Casey is, do we?'

'I do now,' Charlotte smiled. 'Did you hear that ringing sound in the background while Jimmy was talking?'

'I didn't take much notice. Why?'

'Well, it just gave the game away. I was suspicious when he had his arm around my neck earlier. His hands looked like a mechanic's hands. The screwdriver he was carrying was caked in oil, too. But, when I heard that ringing in the background, it confirmed it for me. He's at the scrap yard on White Lund Industrial Estate. Let's go and get that bastard before he even knows we're coming.'

THIRTY-NINE

Morecambe, 1996

It was dark by the time Frank reached Cockerham Sands. He didn't know the area well, and it didn't help that it was so wild outside. He wished he'd come better prepared. Having driven down a narrow country lane, he'd come to an area in the road where a caravan park was signposted at the road end. There was also a wooden footpath sign there, but it was too dark to read it. Frank stepped out of the car, torch in hand, and shone it up at the sign. The abbey was marked from there.

He hesitated a moment. He'd agreed with Casey to meet at the abbey. The sea was wild, the wind was biting off the bay, and it was pitch black along the footpath. Would she have been brave enough to hide out there on her own?

Frank decided to stick to the plan. He shone his torch on the ground and started along the narrow footpath over to the abbey. As he entered the gate which gave access to the track along the top of the beach, a single headlamp shone at him from along the road. He glared at it, but it was too bright to see anything. The glare dazzled him. It was a motorcycle. But, was it Jonny? It made no difference. There was a frightened girl taking refuge over by the abbey. His priority was to ensure her safety. If that had been his own daughter, that's what he would have wanted.

Frank was aware of the motorcycle headlamp disappearing; he wasn't certain in which direction. Either way, if it was Jonny, he hadn't spotted him.

The walk to the abbey in the dark was difficult and uncomfortable. The rain beat in his face, a chill wind cut through his clothing, and he stumbled several times in the darkness. There was sufficient moonlight for him to see the dark silhouette of the abbey up ahead. He called out Casey's name, but his voice was carried away by the gale and the crashing of the waves on the beach.

He reached the abbey at last but could see no signs of Casey. He was aware of a building just beyond the abbey, a farmhouse he thought. He saw a headlamp sweep across its yard, then disappear. Might Casey have gone to the farm?

'Casey?' he called. 'Are you here?'

He walked around the perimeter of the building, shaking the back door firmly. It was locked tight, there was no moving it. As he moved around the far side of the abbey, he tripped over some outer remains of the structure, spraining his ankle and sending his torch flying out into the darkness. He massaged his ankle, cursing his clumsiness. It was sore and difficult to walk on, but he would survive. His torch had struck stones when it had landed. The beam was no longer shining. He picked it up and gave it a shake. He turned it on and off a couple of times. It was dead. The sooner he found Casey and got her out of there, the better.

Frank continued to limp around the far side of the

abbey, expecting Casey's shadow to appear at any moment. She did not seem to be there.

He reached the front of the abbey. There was another wooden door. He gave it a push. He hadn't expected it to move, but it did. Cautiously, he stepped into the abbey. It was almost completely dark in there; his hands were out in front of him so that he could feel his way.

'Casey,' he whispered. At the precise moment that he whispered her name, his hands touched a human form directly in front of him in the darkness. He jumped at the shock of it. There was a scream of panic, and he stepped back and stumbled on his bad ankle. His shirt felt wet.

'PC Allan?'

Casey's voice came weak and scared from the blackness.

'Casey, it's me—'

He heard footsteps.

'Where are you? Are you hurt? I'm so sorry, I was petrified. I thought you were Jonny—'

'I'm hurt, Casey. Did you hit me with something?'

Frank heard sobbing.

'It's okay, Casey, I know you didn't mean to hurt me. I think I've been stabbed. My clothes are wet, I think it's blood—'

Casey was sobbing in the darkness.

'I didn't mean to, PC Allan. I'm so scared. I don't know what to do—'

Frank imagined Kate standing there, a young woman, terrified and vulnerable in the darkness. He felt the wound, assessing the severity, desperately trying to figure out if she'd hit anything that might kill him.

'Casey, it's okay, but you have to stay calm. I'm going to need an ambulance. Reach out your hand, I'm going to give you some coins for a phone box. Go to the farm or find another phone box to call an ambulance. I don't think it's too serious, but I'm losing a lot of blood—'

'Where th'fuck are you, ya little whore?'

Frank could feel Casey tense up, even in the darkness. Jonny was outside. He'd found them. That must have been his headlamp shining at Frank. He must have seen him walking along the footpath. Was that him at the farmyard, circling to head Frank off at the abbey?

Frank could feel himself weakening. His ankle burned, and he pushed on his chest, trying to stop the bleeding.

'Casey,' he whispered. 'Listen to me. I'm going to draw Jonny over here. When I do, sneak out the door and run for your life. Take your motorbike, and go somewhere safe. You've got coins now, so as soon as it's safe, call 999 and get an ambulance out here. Have you got that, Casey? You have to be quiet now. You can do this—'

'I'm so sorry, PC Allan. I've made such a mess of everything. What with Jonny and the baby—'

'Shhh now,' Frank warned her. His eyes had adjusted to the darkness now, and he could make out a large plaque hanging on the wall. He pulled himself over there and rested against the cold stone wall.

'I know yer both in 'ere. Where are you, yer bitch?'

The wooden door creaked open. Frank could see Jonny's silhouette in the doorway. He was carrying something; Frank couldn't figure out what.

'I'm over here, Jonny. Casey has gone. I told her to get out of here.'

Frank followed Jonny's stare in the darkness as he walked over towards the plaque. Frank's eyes flitted from Jonny's silhouette to the moonlit doorway.

'Come on, Casey, get out of here,' he willed her in his mind.

Jonny was standing directly in front of him now. He kicked Frank as if to make certain he wasn't imagining it in the darkness.

'Careful, Jonny, I've hurt my ankle—'

'Like I give a fuck!' Jonny shouted at him.

'I know that you've been bothering that young woman, Jonny—'

He saw Casey slipping out of the door, a silent shadow creeping through the blackness.

'Good girl,' he thought to himself. 'Now go and get me that ambulance.'

'Yer an interfering copper bastard,' Jonny screamed at him. 'That girl was askin' fer it. Whoring around ma lads like that. She gets what she deserves—'

'You've got a daughter, right, Jonny? How would you feel if some man of your age was bothering her?'

If Frank could keep him talking, help would arrive soon.

'I hate ma kids. I hated their bloody mam. That fuckin' woman made ma life hell. Well, she got what the bitch was askin' fer—'

Frank jolted up in his dumped position. Was this Jonny Irving admitting that he'd killed his wife?

'Damn whore's buried in th'back of the bloody garden. The fuckin' kids don't even know their mam is right out there, watchin' o-er them. Stupid fuckers—'

'Did you kill your wife, Jonny?'

There was a flash from out of nowhere, followed by a bang that echoed throughout the small abbey. Frank felt his body convulse. The last words he heard before slipping out of consciousness were in Jonny Irving's contemptuous voice.

'Fuck you, PC Plod.'

FORTY

'Shouldn't we call your DCI friend, first?'

Charlotte was already halfway out the door.

'We will call her. But only when we've taken a closer look. You want to speak to Casey, yes? Well, I have some skin in the game, too. He has my daughter's—'

She paused a moment, wondering how best to describe Milo.

'He has my daughter's boyfriend, too. All I'm suggesting is that we take a look, then call in the police if I'm right. I've learned my lesson from previous experience. I don't want DCI Summers getting half of the Morecambe Police Force over there, if I'm wrong. She needs a win on this case, and I want to help her get it.'

Seth didn't offer any more resistance. He tucked Josh's bike inside the lobby of the guest house, and then, followed Charlotte out the back to her car.

As they were driving, she tried her luck with Seth again. He'd been more forthcoming than when Kate had been asking the questions at Josh's lodge. He'd probably been on the end of enough police interrogations to last a lifetime.

'Were you and Casey close as teenagers?' she chanced.

'We were friends, mainly. Good friends. She was like that with everybody. I wanted it to go further. Then - then everything changed. She got caught up in something. We were having trouble with my dad over a motorbike. Her parents had gone away and left her in the house for the week. She was seventeen, almost eighteen like me. She got into some trouble, and I helped her. She was scared. I helped her to hide from my dad for a while, to let things calm down. We got close then. I think we both needed each other at that time. It wasn't love or anything like that. Not on Gogs' part, anyway.'

Charlotte thought about the Casey that she knew. She was friendly, professional and good fun. If she lived in the resort, they might even have become friends. She'd come back to Morecambe, specifically to make a documentary about events that she had been involved in. She wasn't hiding her name, but at the same time, she wasn't volunteering any information. She'd even asked Charlotte to get the ATC video digitised. She must have known she was on that old footage. Perhaps, she thought nobody would make the connection?

Charlotte's mind was buzzing with possibilities and theories. She didn't want to alienate Seth by pushing him too hard, yet she had a first-hand source sitting right beside her in the car.

'So, who killed David Brewer and Frank Allan? Do you know? Does anybody know?'

Seth looked ahead at the road and didn't turn to face her. She sensed that this might be too much, too soon for him. He answered, anyway.

'I can tell you that none of the four children prosecuted killed David Brewer. Casey didn't kill David Brewer, either, if that's what you're thinking. And, Casey didn't kill Frank Allan, that was just—'

'Casey was involved in Frank Allan's murder? Was she there?'

'I've said enough. I've said too much. I have to speak to Casey first.'

'Is that where the knife wound came from when Frank was murdered? Did Casey do that? It was only shallow, a kitchen knife, or something like that, Kate reckoned. A wound inflicted by an amateur - is that what happened, Seth?'

'Stop the car, please.'

'But, why?'

'This is too much. Just tell me where Gogs is, and I'll make my way there.'

'I'm on your side, Seth. If you were imprisoned for something you didn't do, then the world needs to know about that.'

'We need to let it rest. We've all had our punishments. There's no need to open that can of worms again—'

'But what about DCI Summers, Seth? Doesn't she have a right to know what happened to her father?'

Charlotte took her foot off the accelerator; she was winding herself up and driving too fast. The last thing she needed was to get pulled over.

'She's been in a different sort of prison for the past twenty-five years. Her father was murdered when she was around the same age as you were. You probably passed her in the corridors of the school, even if you didn't know her back then. She never knew who killed her dad. If you or Casey or Jimmy know, doesn't she have a right to hear the truth after all this time? You might be out of prison, but she's still trapped in hers.'

Seth didn't reply. At least, he'd stopped insisting that she stop the car and let him out. She wasn't snooping around that scrapyard without taking somebody who could handle himself if the need arose.

'Let me talk with Casey first. Do you have secrets, Charlotte? I mean secrets which would destroy you if they were ever revealed?'

That was near the knuckle for Charlotte. There was the small matter of Bruce Craven. She was only slightly older than Seth had been when that all played out at the holiday camp. Yet, she couldn't even blame the folly of youth. She'd also colluded with Kate in their witness statements, agreeing that Vinnie Mace had fallen out the back of the wind turbine. He'd stumbled with a bit of help from Kate Summers. But that was their secret, and they'd take it with them to the grave. Is this what had happened to the kids? Is this what the pact was about?

They were turning off into White Lund Industrial Estate now. Charlotte felt a surge of adrenaline, knowing that they were almost at the scrapyard. She checked her phone. It was past five o'clock already.

'Listen, Seth, if there's something you need to get off your chest, you can let DCI Summers know. You've paid an awful price for what happened. If what you say is true - that you're innocent - isn't it time to move on?'

She let it hang in the air. She wanted Seth to mull it over. More than anything, Charlotte was desperate to get the answers that her friend craved so deeply.

Charlotte drove past the entrance of Baker's Breakers and cursed that the main gate was locked up already.

'They finish their working day promptly,' she remarked as she took a left turn into a side road and parked up outside a small catering business that served drinks and snacks to the industrial estate's workers.

'That's odd,' Seth said, craning his neck to look more closely as they drove by. 'There are two scrap cars across the gate. Is that the main entrance?'

'Yes,' Charlotte replied. 'You mean, they're blocking the entrance?'

'Yes, they're in front of the gate. That's weird, isn't it?'

Charlotte switched off the engine and got out of the car.

'We must be able to walk around the fence and get a good look inside. I just want to make sure he's in there. We're going to have to be pretty quick, his live stream is due to start very soon. Kate will have cops all over the place; I'll call her the moment we know he's here.'

Seth pointed as they neared the main gate.

'Look, we can squeeze down that narrow gap between the scrap yard and the next industrial unit. It looks a bit grown over, but we can get through. Are you up for it?'

Charlotte was pleased she'd put her jogging bottoms on. The space between the two fences was overgrown with weeds and small shrubs. However, it gave them direct access to the perimeter fence. Given that the main entrance was so well fortified, it seemed their best chance.

'If he's in here, he must have a way out,' Seth suggested. 'The blocked entrance will stop the police from getting in if they locate him. He must have an escape route out the back. These industrial estates are like rabbit warrens. I'll bet he has it all planned out.'

Charlotte thought Seth had made a good point. If Jimmy was in there, he'd already shown himself to be more than capable of hatching a good escape plan. She didn't think him so daft as to expect that he'd be given free passage to Spain.

They pushed through the weeds and low shrub growth, Seth leading the way and holding back some of the larger obstructions to allow Charlotte to get through without getting snagged. Seth's considerate attitude did not suggest the actions of a teacher-killing psychopath. She had to take him at face value.

The fencing around the scrapyard was mainly constructed of spiked, metal rods. Barbed wire had been placed over the top as an additional fortification. But, as Charlotte and Seth reached the end of that side of the fencing and turned to examine the rear, the metalwork became replaced by six-foot-high, robust wooden fencing. On the other side of the gap was a flimsy wire fence that marked the border of the office block on the other side. Leaning against the wooden fence, concealed by a bush and directly opposite a large hole in the wire fence against which the industrial bins had been placed, was a motorcycle that looked like it had been salvaged from scrap. The engine was still warm from where it had been used recently.

'We've got him,' Charlotte said. 'Now, let's get the cavalry here.'

FORTY-ONE

'Hang on a moment,' Seth interrupted. 'Look, just past that shrub. Those wood slats are loose.'

He walked to the other side of the bush and started to claw at the wood. Several of the slats came away easily, and he rested them against the wire fence at the opposite side. Charlotte joined him so she could take a closer look. She peered into the back of the breaker's yard.

Six feet away from the wooden fence, piled up neatly, was a line of scrap vehicles, two-high. They'd been arranged to allow salvagers and lifting machinery to gain access along the muddy and oily tracks. At the far end of the first row, Charlotte could see a couple of old caravans.

'I'll bet you he's got them in there,' she said as Seth joined her inside the yard.

'Can you smell fuel?' he asked.

'It's a scrapyard, it always smells this way, doesn't it?'

'Not like this, it shouldn't,' Seth replied as he investigated the wooden fence. He gave it a smell.

'That's been doused in petrol,' he said. 'It's recent, too.'

'You don't think he's going to burn the place down, do

you?' Charlotte asked, thinking about Jimmy's long and violent history with fire.

'Let's just give ourselves a bit of insurance,' Seth suggested. He slipped through the gap in the fence and returned wheeling the motorcycle. He walked in the opposite direction, around the edge of the first row of vehicles, and rested it against them.

'There's a second bike there,' he pointed. 'He must have been fixing them up and using them to get about. He's not daft, that's for certain. They both have keys in them.'

'That makes sense. Well, he can't make a fast escape now,' Charlotte remarked, 'So, at least he won't do anything stupid.'

She started walking toward the caravans.

'I don't see him anywhere. Let's see if we can find Milo and Casey. I'm afraid that if the police come in with sirens and the helicopter, he might torch this place. Perhaps we can sneak Casey and Milo out the back?'

Seth looked at her, then ahead to the caravans. He nodded and followed.

Charlotte scanned the scrapyard, trying to get a sense of where they were as she walked along the line of heaped up vehicles.

From the second row onwards, the scrap vehicles were piled three-high. The large crane with the grabber was located three rows in. If Jimmy had blocked the main entrance, that would slow the police. It appeared that he was planning on making his escape out the back. It was a good plan; he'd probably ride straight past the police while they weren't even looking.

They reached the caravans. They were as Bobby Baker had described to her and Kate on their earlier visit: battered, unloved and in need of some superficial repairs. They were, however, no worse than the caravan Bobby was using as his office.

Seth put his finger to his lips and waved Charlotte over. They peered through the filthy window of the first caravan. It was dark, untidy and empty. As Charlotte looked inside, the caravan to their right began to shake. She moved across to take a closer look. She gasped when she saw what was in there, giving Seth a frantic wave to join her.

It was Casey and Milo. Their wrists and ankles were bound by coloured wires which looked like they'd been stripped from the abandoned vehicles. Their mouths were sealed by gaffer tape. Was that the tape from the funeral director's premises? Their eyes were covered with oily rags that looked like they'd been used to clean off vehicle parts.

The entire caravan shook as somebody climbed in at the front. Instinctively, Charlotte and Seth ducked down.

'Okay, pretty boy, it's time to get your gear set up—'

Charlotte and Seth stood to the side, so they could watch without being seen.

Jimmy tore the tape from Milo's mouth.

'Fuck off!' Milo shouted at him.

Jimmy's fist came crashing down on Casey. Seth's body tensed as he heard Casey attempt to shout out through the gaffer tape.

'Every time you open that big gob of yours, your friend will get a thump. Now I know you modern guys are all into women's rights and all that. So, if you don't want her all bruised when she goes on camera, I suggest you shut up.'

Milo was immediately compliant.

'I'm sorry, Casey,' he said.

Jimmy pulled him up and pushed him out of the caravan.

Seth pointed to the side of the caravan and placed his

finger on his lips again. Charlotte stayed close. When the coast was clear, Seth darted out, along the front of the caravan and inside, all the time looking around for Jimmy and Milo. Charlotte was right behind him.

Casey was shaking. She flinched as Seth knelt by her.

'It's okay, Gogs, it's me, Seth.'

He gently removed the rag from around her eyes and warned her that he was going to rip off the tape.

'Oh, God, Charlotte, Seth, he's mad. He wants to put me on camera and make me confess what happened—'

'Woah, steady, Casey. Are you alright?' Charlotte asked. 'Are you hurt?'

'A little. Seth, how did you get here? I thought you'd gone into hiding. I didn't know where you were. It's so good to see you.'

Seth was unfastening the wires from Casey's wrists and ankles. They'd been pulled tight; Charlotte could see deep, red marks where they'd pinched the skin.

'Who is he?' Charlotte asked. 'Do you know who he is?'

'He's Jonny Irving's son,' Casey replied.

'But, Josh is here, in Morecambe. I've spoken to him—' Charlotte started.

'His illegitimate son,' Casey continued. 'He's your half-brother, Seth—'

Seth was looking at her now like she was an apparition.

'I can't believe it's you, Gogs. How can he have an illegitimate son? Even our mum didn't want to be with Jonny. I can't imagine any other woman would go near him.'

'Jimmy was at school, Seth. Don't you remember? He was always messing around with lighters at smoker's corner. He used to nag us to get a ride on the motorbikes when we were over at Heysham Moss. We knew him as Jimmy Rylands. He says his proper name is Jimmy Irving. He reckons Jonny was a great dad to him. He took him to the fair, and even, out on your bike when he stole it from you—'

'I can't cope with this,' Seth replied. 'So, what's his problem? What's this all about?'

Casey looked at Charlotte, then back to Seth.

'He knows about your dad, Seth—'

'What—'

'He knows. That's what all this is about. He wants me to confess.'

'Damn,' Charlotte said. The penny had just dropped. 'You didn't kill David Brewer, did you? You killed Jonny Irving. Jonny killed Brewer, didn't he?'

Seth and Casey looked at each other. Casey nodded.

'He was going to rape me,' Casey said slowly. 'He found me hiding in that old house, and he came for me—'

She stopped.

'I'll bet it was Jimmy who told him about that place. I always wondered how he found me there. I thought only the kids from school knew about it.'

'Were you the one who stabbed Frank Allan?' Charlotte asked.

'Yes,' Casey answered. 'But it was an accident. I'd gone to hide at my granny's caravan at Cockerham Sands. Jonny came after me, and I called Frank Allan. Frank had given me his phone number. He was a good guy. Frank was trying to help me. David Brewer was trying to help me, too. Frank told me to hide when Jonny came for me at Cockerham Sands. I hid in the abbey, away from the caravan. I managed to force the door open. I couldn't see it was Frank Allan when he came inside the abbey. I thought it was Jonny. I stabbed him in self-defence. I panicked. It was dark in there. I swear I didn't kill him—'

'It's okay,' Seth calmed her. 'We need to get you out of here safely—'

'Who did shoot Frank Allan?' Charlotte asked. 'It was Jonny, wasn't it?'

'Yes,' she said, almost inaudibly. 'It was Jonny. He'd got a gun from somewhere. I didn't see it. But, I heard it. I was running across the fields to get away. I called the police from a phone box. I tried to help Frank Allan. But, I was only seventeen, Charlotte. And I was—'

'Pregnant?'

'You know?' Casey asked.

'Seth told me. I'm fitting the pieces together—'

There was a sound to their side over by the entrance. Jimmy climbed up into the caravan, clapping slowly. He stopped and pulled an old gun out of his rear pocket.

'That's Jonny's gun—' Seth began.

'This is perfect,' Jimmy sneered. 'Casey and Seth are both in the same place at the same time. The two murderers who killed my father.'

He pointed the gun at them, and all three drew back, waiting to see what he would do next.

'It's showtime, everyone. Time to let the rest of the world know what you did. And, as for you, Charlotte, I've had enough of you now.'

He pointed the gun directly at her and pulled the trigger.

FORTY-TWO

Charlotte flinched, but the gun did not fire. Jimmy seemed perplexed for a moment. He looked up at Charlotte, who stared into his eyes. She was shaking. She'd had guns pointed at her before, but never at such a close range and with so little opportunity to dodge her assailant.

Then, completely unexpectedly, the gun fired, making Jimmy, Casey and Seth jump with the shock of it. Charlotte let out a scream, and she dropped to the ground.

'Shit,' Jimmy said, taken aback by what had just happened. 'This fucking gun is useless—'

'Jesus, Jimmy, what have you done?' Seth shouted.

'Oh my God, Charlotte—,' Casey screamed, trying to make her way over to the slumped body despite being bound.

'Get away from her!' Jimmy commanded, waving the gun at Seth and Casey. They backed off, wary of an unhinged Jimmy and watching a small pool of blood form at the side of Charlotte.

'We're going out there; it's time to tell the truth. Get up, go!'

Jimmy pointed the gun as he motioned to Casey that she should stand up and walk.

'You try anything, and I shoot,' Jimmy warned.

Charlotte opened her eyes. The pain was excruciating, but the misfire had struck the side of her leg. It had caught her so much by surprise that she'd instinctively dropped to the ground. Hearing the panic in Jimmy's voice, she played dead. She could feel the blood pooling around her leg, and it hurt like hell, but she could still move it, and she was alive. It was the only play she had left, their options seemed suddenly depleted.

She was about to pull herself up and examine her wound when the caravan sunk from the weight of somebody coming inside. She lay still again, partially opening her eyes, so she could see what was going on. Jimmy threw Milo into the caravan and locked the door. His head was bloody; it looked like he'd been struck.

Hearing Jimmy's voice shouting commands to Casey and Seth in the distance, Charlotte got up and limped over to Milo, who was groaning. Seeing Charlotte, he roused himself.

'Are you okay?' Charlotte whispered.

'I heard a gun—,' Milo began.

'He shot me, but it's not too bad. I can walk—'

'Damn, Charlotte. You need to get some pressure on that.'

She looked down. It was painful and worse to look at. It had gone through her jogging bottoms, tearing the flesh at the top of her leg.

'Here, take my T-shirt; I can secure it with this wire—'

'Can you smell burning?' Charlotte interrupted.

The two of them looked around.

'For Christ's sake, he's set fire to the outside of the caravan!' Milo cursed.

He was up on his feet immediately. He picked up a small, metal stool that was tucked underneath the wooden table at the far end of the caravan and smashed the window. It broke easily, allowing Milo to clear out the remainder of the shards.

'Take my hand, Charlotte,' he urged, grabbing Charlotte and pulling her up. 'You go first,' he said, picking up the wire and discarded T-shirt to take with him. Charlotte grunted with pain as he helped her to climb out of the window. Her ribs burned, her leg was raw, but she knew she could carry on, it wouldn't beat her. They were at the rear of the scrapyard, out of sight of Jimmy, but caught in a cluster of old caravans which were all dumped close together.

'Here,' Milo said as he passed the T-shirt and wire to Charlotte through the window. There was a massive whoosh as the front of the caravan ignited, and the flames took their hold. Charlotte helped Milo through the window. He'd been struck hard on his head; he was bleeding, too.

'If we go right around the back of these caravans, we can take cover by the rear fence and get some help,' Charlotte suggested, as she led the way from the burning caravan clear of the flames. They located the perimeter fence and followed it so that they could navigate back to where Charlotte and Seth had found their way in.

'Sit down here,' Milo said, finding an old fuel can which had been tucked in next to a car. Charlotte smelt it before sitting down.

'He's set this place to burn,' she said. 'Seth and I could smell petrol when we came in. I think he's leaving his signature trail before he runs off.'

Charlotte sat on the overturned can, and Milo wrapped the T-shirt around her wound.

'I'm going to pull this tight to try and stop the bleeding,' he warned.

Milo took the first piece of wire, wrapped it around Charlotte's leg and the T-shirt, then twisted it around. He turned the ends a couple of times until it dug in tightly. He then repeated what he'd done at the bottom of the T-shirt. Charlotte gasped as he pulled the wires together firm and tight, but she knew enough about first aid to know that this was all they could do, given the resources at their fingertips.

'Do you have your phone?' Charlotte asked as he finished.

'No, Jimmy has it. He's using it for his live stream.'

Charlotte felt in her pocket. She still had her device. She speed-dialled Kate's number. It rang twice, and Kate picked up.

'Charlotte? Are you at home still?'

'It's a long story, you need to listen. I'm at Baker's Breaker's—'

'Jesus, Charlotte!'

'Jimmy has Seth and Casey—'

She checked her phone. It was five minutes until six o'clock.

'He's got them ready for his live stream. He has a gun, Kate—'

'Are you hurt?'

'He shot me, but I'll survive—'

'For Christ's sake, Charlotte—'

'We haven't got time. I think the gun is the one that was used to kill your dad, Kate. He's blocked the gates, you won't get in that way. He's also set the place to go up in flames. I don't know what his game is, or how he intends to get out. He's gone crazy, Kate, be careful. Get an ambulance here, Milo is hurt too—'

'How many of you are down there?'

'Me, Milo, Casey and Seth. Everybody is fine, so far. Jimmy's got that crazy look in his eyes. He's set fire to the caravans already—'

'Stay on the line, Charlotte-'

Charlotte listened as Kate issued quickfire instructions to her team in the office. She caught the gist of it. Firearms officers were to be dispatched, the police helicopter was being launched, all units were heading that way, and the fire service and ambulance were being called over. At any moment, the sirens would begin to fill the air, and Jimmy would know his time was up.

'Are you still there, Charlotte?'

'Yes, I'm here. I take it you're not buying his plane ticket to Spain, then?'

'You have to get out of there. It's not your job to sort this out. We'll get officers in there—'

'There's only one way in, as far as I can tell. You won't get in the front gates, even if you cut open the padlock. You may get officers in, but not vehicles. We found an exit at the back, but be careful, it stinks of petrol. I think he may have set the place to burn—'

'Do not engage Jimmy, Charlotte, leave that to the firearms officers—'

'What about Seth and Casey? I think he'll kill them after he gets his damn confession—'

'Leave them to us, Charlotte—'

Before Kate had finished her sentence, Milo sprang up and shouted at Charlotte.

'Get down!' he yelled, pushing her off the petrol can

and covering her on the ground with his body. A huge fire-ball shot into the air, as the caravans went up in a mass of flames, glass blowing out of their windows and debris landing all around them.

FORTY-THREE

'He piled gas canisters by that beaten-up caravan at the rear. I just saw it in time as the flames reached them.'

Milo had rolled off Charlotte and was dusting debris off his clothes.

'Jimmy's gone mad,' Charlotte said, looking around, taking in the situation around her. 'He's been so calm and level-headed through everything, now it feels like he's raging out of control.'

She looked for her phone. It had flown out of her hand when Milo rushed to protect her from the blast.

'I think my phone's in there somewhere,' she indicated, pointing towards the scrap vehicles piled up directly behind them.

'What's the plan?' Milo asked, looking around as if searching for ideas.

'Kate wants us to get out of here and leave it to the police,' Charlotte replied.

Already, even over the roar of the flames, they could hear the sound of sirens in the distance.

'They'll be here very soon,' Milo observed. 'How did you get in?'

Charlotte pointed over to the fence where the planks were rested at the side of the gap.

'We can nip out the back and join the police at the front—'

As she started speaking, the entire rear fence was engulfed by a wave of flames as sparks jumped from the burning caravans to the fuel-drenched structure. The fire ran from the caravan side of the yard across to the far end, like some sinister pyrotechnics display. The two of them reared back, pressing their backs against the bodywork of the scrap vehicles to their rear.

'Shit! Quick, if we're getting out this way, we'd better do it now,' Charlotte shouted.

They moved over to where she and Seth had got in and leaned the planks of wood that they'd placed to the side, Charlotte gritting her teeth through the pain of her wounded leg.

'Jimmy must have soaked the base of the fence with the petrol from that fuel can,' Milo suggested. The flames took a grasp of the dry wood fast; the small gap in the fence was ablaze already.

'I'm not going through there,' Milo continued. 'We'll get burned, for sure.'

Charlotte looked at it. She didn't fancy her chances, either. Besides, it was a fire. She'd rather do battle with anything but flames.

'Pass me that windscreen wiper by your foot,' Charlotte urged.

Milo looked down. Cast aside on the ground was a long windscreen wiper, discarded from the van that was partially crushed to their side. Milo handed it over.

Charlotte used it to hook the loose planks off the side of the fence, so they crashed to the ground, clear of the rapidly growing flames.

'Stamp out the flames,' Charlotte continued.

'What are you doing?' Milo asked, as he carried out her instructions.

'Being as crazy as Jimmy,' she answered. 'Just investing in a bit of insurance.'

Milo looked at her. He hadn't got a clue what she was talking about, but he did as he was told. They rescued four of the sturdy wooden planks which were only mildly singed, due to their distance from the main fire. The fence was now a tower of roaring flames, the heat was becoming too intense to bear.

'Take two planks, and head for the end,' Charlotte coughed. The smoke was filling the air now; they had to get out of there. They took the planks and ran to the end of the row of scrap cars, up to where the two motorcycles had been placed.

'You're not planning to use these, are you?' Milo asked. From the look on his face, Charlotte reckoned he'd worked out her plan.

'Do you know who Evel Knievel is?' she asked.

Milo's face was blank.

'Of course, you don't. He was a stunt motorcyclist when I was a kid. We used to have this toy where we made him jump over stuff. It was amazing—'

'You're not going to do that? We'll kill ourselves. I've never even been on a motorcycle before—'

'Me, neither. Well, I have. Sort of. It was a small one. I stole it from somebody. Anyhow, we're not the ones who are making the jump. Casey and Seth are going to do it—'

'You're bloody mad. Lucia said you're crazy. In a good

way, of course. Aren't you supposed to be attending PTA meetings and doing embroidery? No sexism intended. No ageism intended, either—'

'Screw that, Milo. I'm not burning in here. I'm not going to leave Seth and Casey, either. You figured out what happened to Frank Allan, didn't you?'

'Yes, I did. It had to be Jonny Irving. Everything points to Jonny. I did my research. Nobody knows what happened to him. I do. The kids killed him—'

'What?'

'Yup. The kids killed him. They were protecting Casey—'

'So, why was there no body found?'

'That's the bit I can't explain. Casey confirmed it, though she didn't kill Jonny. Or Brewer, come to that.'

The flames were getting closer now; they were flaring up close to the scrap vehicles.

'This whole bloody scrapyard is going up, if we're not careful,' Charlotte warned. 'Let's move this stuff out the way.'

They wheeled the motorcycles three rows of cars up, Charlotte moving as fast as she could with her wound, then retrieved the salvaged planks. As they turned their backs on the fencing, one of the vehicles halfway down the row ignited. Charlotte looked overhead. The police helicopter had arrived.

'Casey asked Brewer to meet her at the abandoned house. Brewer got there just after Jonny arrived. Casey said Brewer tried to protect her, but he had an epileptic fit and collapsed. Jonny hit him on the head with a hammer that the kids had stolen from school so that Casey could protect herself while she was hiding away in the old house. I reckon Jimmy must have told him about the old house. Only the school kids and the cops knew about it. That's why Jimmy knows half of what went on. One minute, he sends Jonny to find Casey in the wrecked house; the next, the man he calls his dad disappears. So, who does he blame? Jonny must have burned Brewer's body and wiped the hammer of his prints, which is how the kids got the blame. Either that, or he was wearing gloves—'

'So, they took the heat over Brewer to cover up the fact they'd killed Jonny?'

'Something like that. I think the kids thought Casey had killed Brewer—'

'Who got rid of Jonny's body? The kids can't have done that?'

'That's the final mystery - fucking hell!'

The tower of cars closest to the burning fence was now well alight, and one of the vehicles had just exploded, sending a shower of broken glass across the yard.

'We have to get to Casey and Seth,' said Charlotte. 'Where are they?'

'Follow me,' Milo replied, leading the way.

They passed another two rows of stacked vehicles, then Milo ducked down a pathway and crouched behind another row of vans.

'Over there,' he nodded.

Standing in front of Milo's camera rig were Jimmy, Casey and Seth. Seth and Casey were on their knees directly in front of Jimmy, who had the gun pointing at their heads. Jimmy looked deranged and was shouting at the camera.

'He's going to get them to say what happened—,' Milo began.

'What do you know about Jonny Irving?' Charlotte asked.

'He was a bastard. It sounds like he got what he deserved.'

'I think the kids have served their time, don't you?'

'Yes, I do,' Milo replied. 'They've more than served their time. Seth was stitched up by that national newspaper, and they received poor legal advice. Seth is the biggest loser here. I think he was protecting Casey from something—'

Charlotte knew exactly what he was protecting her from; the prospect of going to prison whilst carrying their baby.

'So, we're agreed. Nobody gives a shit about what happened to Jonny Irving. And, they've all had their punishment, yes?'

'Agreed,' Milo said.

'Right, I want you to make your way over to that grabber crane over there. These people seem to leave the keys in everything. Start it up, and cause a distraction—'

'Where are you going, Charlotte?'

'I'm going to screw up Jimmy's presentation—'

'Jesus, Lucia said you were like this—'

'If we're all getting out of here, this is what it's going to take.'

Milo nodded and started to move off.

'Milo!' Charlotte shouted after him.

'What?'

'You're a good kid. Lucia could have done much worse than getting together with you. I'm sorry I gave you a hard time.'

'Thanks, Charlotte,' he beamed at her. 'Let's do this.'

Charlotte gave Milo some time to get ahead of her, then limped over to the clearing in the cars where Jimmy, Seth and Casey were standing. Overhead, she could hear the buzz of the police helicopter. She did a double-take as she spotted a drone hovering overhead. Although the rear of the scrapyard was engulfed by flames and smoke, she could still see the flashing lights of police and emergency vehicles up ahead at the entrance to the yard. She knew how this would work from previous experience. There would be a fast assessment of the scene, then they'd take action. Kate knew there were four of them in there with Jimmy. They would seek to preserve lives at all costs.

'Give it up, Jimmy,' she shouted.

He stopped dead and looked at her. Charlotte could see the live stream was going ahead by the illuminated light on Milo's equipment.

'I'm beginning to think it's impossible to kill you, Charlotte Grayson,' Jimmy scowled.

'Have you told everybody it was your father, Jonny Irving, who killed David Brewer?' Charlotte taunted. 'Have you let everybody into the biggest secret? That Jonny also killed an innocent police officer using that very gun you're holding in your hand?'

'You're talking rubbish,' he screamed at her. 'Casey stabbed and shot Frank Allan at Cockersand Abbey. She stole the gun from Jonny's garage. She lured him there and murdered him—'

Jimmy's version of the story absolved his father. He was delusional now. Charlotte put him right.

'Jonny struck David Brewer with a hammer that the children had stolen from the school so that Casey would have a weapon to protect herself from him. He tried to assault her—'

'You're talking nonsense. The kids murdered David Brewer, the whole of Morecambe knows that—'

From nowhere, a massive iron grabber crashed to the ground directly to the side of Jimmy, Casey and Seth. It still had a crushed car in its teeth. It sent dirt and car debris all over. Seth rolled to his side and kicked Jimmy's feet from underneath him. Jimmy fell, dropping the gun. Jimmy moved swiftly, attempting to climb to his feet. The iron grabber started to move upwards, and instinctively, as Seth tried to bring down Jimmy while his hands were still bound, Jimmy grabbed the exhaust pipe of the scrap car so that he could swing himself out of the way.

Whatever Milo was doing on the controls took everybody by surprise. The grabber raised suddenly with Jimmy still hanging on. Charlotte watched Jimmy as he looked down, considering for a moment whether to let go of the exhaust. He was now suspended over a wall of exploding vehicles; he hung on for dear life as Milo raised him high above the flames and left him dangling there. As each explosion fired, a new row of scrap vehicles ignited around them. The entire scrapyard seemed like it was now engulfed in flames.

Milo appeared, looking pleased with himself. He looked up at Jimmy dangling from the car's exhaust, and gave him the finger.

'Sorry about that first crash, I was trying to figure out the controls. He'll be safe enough up there until the cops get him, won't he?'

'We need to untie them,' Charlotte screamed at him, watching how easily the flames were now spreading. If they didn't move fast, Jimmy would be the only one who did make it out alive. Milo and Charlotte removed the bindings from Seth and Casey.

'This way,' Charlotte motioned, leading them towards the motorbikes. Seth and Casey were sore and stiff, but they followed Charlotte to the motorcycles. They looked like the walking wounded as they moved along, each nursing different injuries. There were more explosions across the scrapyard. With each explosion, a new row of scrap vehicles would ignite. They were caught in the teeth of hell.

Charlotte reeled as she glimpsed a flashback to her friend, deep within the bales of the haystack. Charlotte had urged her to go back along her own tunnel, but she'd panicked and taken a wrong route. She heard the dying screams of her friend echoing in the flames all around them. Nobody else was dying like that while she had anything to do with it.

'We're jumping the fence!' she shouted at Casey and Seth.

'What?' they asked.

'I haven't ridden in years—' Seth protested.

'I stopped riding bikes when we left Morecambe—,' Casey added.

'We jump that fence, or we die here,' Charlotte pushed. 'If we jump the rear fence, there's an empty car park on the other side. We can do this. We have to—'

'Fuck it, let's do it,' Seth replied, looking at Casey. He and Casey moved over to the motorcycles, taking one each and examining the controls.

'Milo, quick, we need to make ramps,' Charlotte continued.

They dragged the planks of wood over towards the rear fence, which was still burning.

'Here, help me with this oil drum—'

There were three empty oil drums placed against the perimeter fence and surrounded by heaped-up debris. They each rolled one over and placed it a short distance from the burning wooden fence. The planks were rested on top, two on each, creating a solid ramp. Charlotte placed loose bricks in front of each oil drum, in case they rolled. Each movement sent a searing pain through her injured leg, but it was not so bad that she couldn't carry on.

Still, cars were exploding and bursting into flames throughout the entire scrapyard, and the police helicopter buzzed overhead, as if the team inside didn't know what to do about the situation below.

Casey and Seth fired up their motorcycles. Both were revving madly, the petrol fumes filling the small pathway at the far side of the scrapyard.

'Are the angles right?' Charlotte asked.

'We'll soon find out,' Seth replied. 'Come on, get on the back of the bikes. The flames are becoming too intense. If one of these cars explodes, we're done for.'

Milo clambered on the bike behind Casey, wrapping his arms around her waist.

'Hey, Casey,' Charlotte shouted over. 'Nobody needs to know about Jonny Irving. Nobody is looking for him. Okay?'

Casey looked Charlotte directly in the face.

'Okay,' she replied, 'This all ends here.'

She revved the motorcycle, took it as far up the path at the side of the iron fencing as safely as she could, then began the run at the ramp. Charlotte watched her racing directly at it.

'Turn to the right when you land,' she shrieked as Casey rode by. Casey flew up the ramp; the bike hurtled through the air with Milo hanging on for dear life. They cleared the fence but disappeared into the thick, black smoke.

'Okay, our turn,' Seth said. 'Get on the back—'

'Get the bike ready. I'll be back—' Charlotte replied.

Charlotte limped back to where Jimmy had been live streaming. She picked up the gun, which had been discarded on the floor. Clasping it firmly, she rushed back to

Seth, who was revving the engine of his motorcycle and ready to go. Charlotte climbed on the back.

'I'm taking the evidence. I meant what I said,' Charlotte started, 'Nobody needs to know about your dad. He's gone, it's over. You've had your punishment. It's time for you to get on with the rest of your life.'

'Hold tight,' Seth warned. The bike set off with a spin of the back wheel. He steadied it quickly, lining up with the ramps up ahead. As they raced towards the oil drums, a flare of flames erupted from a crushed van to their left-hand side.

'Fuck!' Seth cursed as he instinctively swerved to avoid it, narrowly missing the iron fence on his right, then forcing the steering back so that they'd hit their target.

They struck the ramp at an angle, flying into the air, directly into the wall of smoke.

'Veer to the right, or you'll smack into the building,' Charlotte warned, as she closed her eyes and clung on tight to Seth's waist. The motorcycle thumped onto the ground. Seth veered severely to the right, narrowly avoiding the office block and applying the brakes just in time to bring it to halt in front of the wire fence.

'Fuck!' he screamed. 'Fuck, we did it!'

Cautiously, Charlotte opened her eyes and looked over towards the scrapyard. Through the smoke, she could just make out Jimmy, still clinging to the exhaust pipe of the suspended car, towers of flames below him. The crane had caught fire now, and the car which was suspended in the great iron clasps was now alight. The last thing she saw before a police vehicle raced into the empty car park of the office block was the vehicle exploding into a ball of fire, with Jimmy being instantly consumed by the flames which had fascinated him for so much of his life.

EPILOGUE

'And, the winner of the Regional Journalist of the Year is—'

'I feel more nervous now than I did when Vinnie Mace was chasing me on that jet-ski,' Charlotte whispered to Will. She couldn't believe they were there. Not only was it the Savoy Hotel in London, but Alex Kennedy was on the stage, presenting the prizes. As the former presenter of the Crime Beaters TV programme, she was crime reporting royalty as far as Charlotte was concerned.

A sound effect of a drum roll resounded through the room, and Alex Kennedy made a big deal of slowly opening an oversized, golden envelope.

'I wish Kate had managed to get here. I'll be disappointed if I win, and she doesn't see me stumbling on stage in these damn high heels. They're staying on until this bit is over, then I'm putting my flats back on—'

'There she is,' Will pointed. 'She's waving from the far end of the room—'

Alex Kennedy put everyone out of their misery.

'—Charlotte Grayson from The Bay View Weekly for her work on Morecambe's Missing Children—'

Charlotte's table erupted into applause. All around her, her family, friends and colleagues stood up, delighted for her success. She looked around the table; she couldn't have been happier to see all those faces. Will, Lucia and Olli were there, and Teddy had allowed them to bring along Willow and Milo, mainly due to a deal he'd struck with Milo to share content between the newspaper and Internet-Revelations.tube. Casey had also managed to tag along at Charlotte's request, after making a separate arrangement with Teddy to include newspaper source material in her finished documentary. The table of ten was completed by Nigel and Teddy, with an empty seat, awaiting Kate.

Teddy had been canny; he understood well how bringing all the protagonists to a media event in a case that had attracted national interest could only mean lots of coverage for the local paper. If anybody could make the newspaper survive the slings and arrows of the internet, it would be Teddy.

'Get yourself up there, this is your moment,' Will said, kissing Charlotte on her cheek and squeezing her around her waist.

Charlotte took a deep breath, concentrated on balancing in her heels, and walked up confidently to the stage. She'd been practising, just in case. Her leg had healed well enough from the gunshot wound and she was determined to walk on that stage without any trace of a limp. As she made her way up the steps, she was aware of the entire room applauding and cheering. She'd never experienced anything quite like it in her life. The closest she'd come to an accolade like this was winning the prize for the neatest handwriting at primary school, and that was a skill that was now long gone.

As Charlotte crossed the stage, bathed in the beam of a

spotlight that had followed her from her seat, Alex read out details of why the prize had been awarded. She caught the gist of it, as phrases like, *incisive reporting, empathetic writing,* and *immersive description,* were used. Alex shook her hand and leaned in for a hug.

'Great work,' Alex whispered to her. 'I'll try and catch you later, if I can. I'm here with Peter Bailey; he has a connection to your area. It would be great to catch up.'

'Sure, I'd love to,' Charlotte replied.

Alex passed over the small trophy then stood back and allowed Charlotte to step up to the microphone.

This is just like a school assembly, she told herself. *Just imagine it's a hall full of kids, and you're handing out the class awards for the week.*

She paused a moment, wanting to take it all in. The room was packed with the great and good of the media world, from TV, radio, internet and newspapers. There were national stars there: bloggers, podcasters, and tables packed with reporters, producers and journalists. Will was beaming so much, he was in danger of outshining the spotlight. Nigel put up his thumb, and it made her smile and relax.

'Thank you so much for this award—' she began. 'I've worked with some amazing people who helped me along the way. First, I'd like to thank Nigel Davies from The Bay View Weekly whose fault it is that I ever started working in journalism—'

Nigel let out a loud whoop, and there was a ripple of laughter across the room.

'I'd also like to thank Teddy Solomon for having the faith to bring on new and raw talent at The Bay View Weekly, even when they haven't yet submitted all the essays for their correspondence course—'

There was more laughter. As Charlotte paused for it to die down, she watched as Kate took her seat at the table. She couldn't wait to speak to her friend.

'I must thank my friends and family who have had to be around while I've been involved in events which, quite frankly, a woman of my age should know better than to get caught up in—'

There was more laughter. It was a supportive crowd. Comedy was not Charlotte's sweet spot, but for a room of hardened journalists, they were on their best behaviour.

'Finally, I want to take a moment to remember the victims. While I'm receiving this award, there are people whose lives have been ruined by the criminals that I write about. As I tuck another story in my portfolio and you fold up a newspaper and throw it in the recycling, these victims have to pick up the pieces of their lives and somehow move on after the most traumatic events. In accepting this award, from one rookie reporter to a room full of pros, I would urge you to never forget the victims of the stories you write about. Thank you.'

There was a huge round of applause and a standing ovation. Alex Kennedy moved in and gave Charlotte a second hug.

'Hey, I've got to follow that now,' she smiled at Charlotte. 'Well done, that was a great acceptance speech.'

Charlotte made her way off the stage, holding her award up high so that everybody could see it, and the photographers got their shot. It took her ten minutes to make it back to her table, what with people she didn't even know stopping her along the way to congratulate her on her reporting. When she finally made it back to the table, there were hugs, kisses, cheers and congratulations all around. Teddy ordered more champagne, and eventually, the awards were concluded, and the food started being served.

'I thought you weren't going to make it,' Charlotte said to Kate as she tucked into her starter. She hadn't a clue what it was, but it tasted delicious.

'I'm so sorry,' Kate replied, 'but I wanted to be able to tie up some loose ends for you. This seemed like the right time to deliver good news.'

'As if an award wasn't enough for one night,' Charlotte smiled.

'You're going to like this. First, I want to thank you. I'm so grateful, Charlotte. The forensics team managed to match the markings on the bullet they took out of my father with the barrel of Jimmy's gun. It was Jonny Irving who shot my father. Casey has confirmed everything we need to know about that night.'

'I'm so pleased for you, Kate. After all these years.'

She hugged Kate hard. It was hard to imagine what her friend had been through, not knowing who had killed her father for all those years. And losing her brother too; it must have taken immense strength to get on with her life after those events.

'Is anything going to be done about Jonny Irving?' Charlotte asked.

'Nobody cares what happened to him,' Kate replied. 'Nobody has reported him missing. Everybody was glad to see the back of him. We even tracked down Jimmy's mother in Spain. She couldn't care less what had happened to Jonny, and she'd disowned her son years ago. She even thought Jimmy might have killed him.'

'Imagine nobody caring if you're alive or dead. So, nothing will be pursued over Jonny Irving?'

'No, that chapter remains closed. He's officially my

father's murderer, and he's assumed dead, but with no body and no leads, nobody is asking any more questions.'

'So, what delayed you today?' Charlotte asked. 'You said you were going to see somebody.'

'Yes,' Kate replied. She lowered her voice. 'Look, Charlotte, I know you and I already have secrets. And I know we're adding a new one to the list, as a result of this case. I went to see Larry Schofield today—'

'Is he okay now?'

'Yes, he's living on his friend's boat until the insurance sorts him out. He wanted to confess, Charlotte—'

'Oh - what did he say?'

'I know you know what happened to Jonny Irving. I'll bet Milo does, too. I don't care. The bastard killed my father, and my superiors aren't investigating his disappearance any further.'

'So, what did Larry say?'

'He wanted to confess something. You were right about his lying about that leg wound—'

'I knew it!'

'A few days after my dad's body was found at Cockersand Abbey, on the night David Brewer died, Larry happened to see the four children in the vicinity of the old house where Brewer's body was found. He thought nothing of it at first but returned to check out the house before the police got there. He got an uneasy feeling about seeing the kids after a conversation he'd had with my dad earlier that day. He didn't see Brewer's corpse, but he did find Jonny's dead body badly concealed under some plastic sheeting and waste at the back of the building, in the yard. He put two and two together and figured the kids had killed Jonny. With what he knew about him, he didn't blame them. He also thought Jonny had killed my dad, but there were no suspects or evidence, so it looked like he'd get away with it.'

'So?'

'In short, Larry disposed of the body. He borrowed a friend's motorboat from Glasson Dock and dropped it out at sea, weighed down by rocks. He caught his leg on the motor when Jonny's body got snagged on the side of the boat, and he had to slip into the water to pull it off. He always thought they might find the body eventually, but they never did.'

'Wow,' Charlotte said, shocked by this information. It filled in the final gap. And, it made complete sense.

'He was ready to hand himself in and confess,' Kate continued.

'I hope you talked him out of it?' Charlotte checked.

'Of course, what would be the point? Jonny deserved it, nobody's looking for him, the world is a better place without him. I feel sorry for Jimmy, though.'

'Me, too,' Charlotte agreed. 'I mean, he was a psycho, but he wasn't motivated by personal gain like the usual sociopaths are. He loved Jonny. He wanted justice for him—'

'Here's my award-winning journalist—'

Teddy interrupted them. He'd drunk a little too much champagne and was enjoying the most attention that the paper had garnered in some time.

'So, have you thought about the job offer?' he asked. 'I'm serious. I want you reporting on The Bay View Weekly.'

'Will and Nigel, you might as well listen in on this,' Charlotte said, nudging her husband to get his attention.

'I've made a big decision. Now we've sold the guest house and bought the house in Hest Bank that we wanted, I've decided that I'm not going to work for the newspaper—'

There were gasps of surprise and disappointment from

Teddy and Nigel. Will rested his hand on hers to offer his support.

'I've been offered a writing deal to tell the true story of the Morecambe Four. It comes with a decent advance. I'm co-authoring it with Josh. Seth and Eric have agreed to help, too—'

'And, Robbie?' Milo asked.

'He requested to keep his anonymity,' Kate chipped in. 'He's happy doing whatever it is he's doing, and he wants it to stay that way. He was interviewed by the police to confirm the details of David Brewer's murder, but he gets to keep his new identity secret, and he wants it to stay that way.'

'Well, I wish you nothing but luck,' Teddy said. 'I've never seen the newspaper's circulation so high in years, so you've done great work already. Many thanks.'

'I'll miss you,' Nigel added. 'It seems no time at all since I came to photograph you both outside the guest house. Who bought the guest house, by the way?'

'Oh, some investment company,' Will answered. 'It means that Isla and George can retire without a backward glance, and Piper and Agnieszka can get on with their lives. Jenna and Piper are going to open a small tea shop on the promenade with some business start-up funding. Agnieszka has her citizenship fully resolved now and can get proper funding for her studies. We're delighted for her.'

'What about Rex Emery?' Nigel asked. 'Wasn't he going to take it over?'

'He's seen good sense,' Charlotte chipped in. 'He finally realised that he's best making a clean start. He gave us his blessing over the sale.'

Will and Nigel returned to their previous conversation, and Teddy wandered off in search of more champagne.

'I have news of my own,' Kate whispered.

'More news?' Charlotte replied. 'I'm not certain I can take any more surprises.'

'I've applied for a transfer. To Hull, of all places.'

'Hull? Why?'

'I went to university there after Dad died, and before returning to the police in Morecambe. I like it there. With everything that's happened, I want a fresh start. It's hard to carry all these secrets about on your own doorstep. It's the right thing, I think.'

'Good luck, Kate. I'll miss you if you go. You've been such a good friend.'

The starters were now being cleared and preparations being made for the main meal.

'I'm just nipping to the ladies,' Charlotte announced to Kate.

'I'll come with you,' Casey called from across the table. 'I'd like a quick word.'

Charlotte smiled at her, and they wove their way through the array of tables and groups of chatting journalists.

'I want to thank you for keeping quiet about Jonny,' Casey whispered when she was certain they had the lavatories to themselves. 'Those boys killed Jonny to protect me. It was a fierce fight, he was like an animal. It was more self-defence than it was murder. I don't know how they even brought him down. If they hadn't killed him, he would have killed all of us, I'm certain of it. I can never repay them for what they did for me. Seth refused to have our baby born in custody. I owe them a lot for that pact. They took the blame for Brewer, knowing they had killed Jonny. Maybe I can repay them now, by telling their story. Without the bit about them killing Jonny, of course. That's our secret.'

'What about you and Seth?' Charlotte wondered.

'He is the father of my son. There's no relationship there between us, too many years have passed. We weren't in love at the time, it was just a thing that happened. But, I want him to know his son. He ended up giving away twenty-five years of his freedom for me, due to that bloody newspaper and some bad legal advice. I owe him that.'

'Your secret is safe with me,' Charlotte reassured her.

'By the way, where did the fuel come from that was used to burn Brewer? I've been trying to figure that out.

'It's no big mystery,' Casey replied. 'Seth brough a can of fuel round to the old house so I could get a fire going easily. Jonny must have panicked. I guess he torched Brewer after he killed him.'

They headed off to their cubicles, and Casey had moved on by the time Charlotte emerged to wash her hands. A woman was standing at the sinks, checking her make-up in the mirror.

'Charlotte Grayson, congratulations again!'

It was Alex Kennedy, the host of the awards, taking a moment out of the limelight.

'I hear on the grapevine you've had some quite amazing adventures,' Alex smiled at her. 'We have a friend in common, too. DCI Kate Summers was involved in our little adventure. She's a good person to have on your side.'

Charlotte had read a little of Alex's story. Peter Bailey had been a local journalist until moving with Alex to Spain. Nigel had mentioned that he knew him.

'Well, it's all over for me now. I'm retiring from newspapers before I even begin. A young internet influencer has persuaded me that there's no future in the old-style media. I'm working for myself and becoming a journalist-author.

It's safer that way. I won't get into any more trouble. I've had enough scrapes and bruises to last a lifetime.'

Alex looked at her and smiled.

'You know, I don't think you ever truly leave this profession, Charlotte. News stories have a habit of finding you when you're a journalist. Let's meet up for a drink after they finish serving the food. I'll tell you about my own adventure with Pete. One minute you think you're safely out of the profession, and the next, you never know what's coming around the corner.'

Charlotte nodded and agreed to meet up after the food had been served. She was in no rush to ride into the eye of the storm anytime soon. But, she liked to think her adventures weren't completely over.

Read about Alex Kennedy, Pete Bailey, DCI Summers and Steven Terry in the Don't Tell Meg Trilogy.

AUTHOR NOTES

Now you know how all those loose ends tie-up. You didn't think I was going to kill Charlotte, did you? After nine books and over half a million words of the Morecambe Bay series, that would be too harsh if you've followed her from Left For Dead through to Last To Tell.

I've loved writing these three trilogies. When I started to write Left For Dead, that was originally going to be a standalone novel. Once I'd written it, I thought to myself *What if Jenna got a knock at the door and it wasn't all over?* From that point onwards, the story took care of itself.

So, is this it for Charlotte? The answer is, I'm afraid, yes. She may well re-appear in future books as a secondary character, but I think for the sake of realism and finishing at the right time, that's quite enough adventure for Charlotte.

However, I am considering taking on the character of DCI Kate Summers in future, though if I do, she will have relocated to Hull, a city where I spent seven years of my BBC radio career.

I feel like a change of location and some new cases to solve is just what Kate needs. As a journalist, Hull offered a rich tapestry of city and rural news stories, with heavy industry, a large passenger and freight port, and some memories of the big stories that I covered whilst reporting there. There's also the Humber Bridge as a major landmark, a rich history of fishing, the unique Hull Fair, and a wonderful coastline offering news and unexplored seaside locations.

As a writer, this book gave me a bit of a problem. I couldn't have Charlotte just standing up and walking away from her near-death experience, so I needed to build in some recovery time for her. I've just watched a series on Netflix where one minute the detective is having the life beaten out of her, the next minute she's up on two feet without pain or a groan. The way I got around this was by bringing Josh and Seth into the story, turning the heat up for Milo and Casey, and dropping DCI Comfort right in the middle of it with his indiscreet social media message. It gives Charlotte just enough time to take on some light duties and get a bit of bed rest before she has to cope with her grand finale.

It was great to reveal Frank Allan's backstory in this trilogy. Frank's demise was almost a throwaway comment by Brett in the second trilogy, but setting the events of this book in the past again allowed me to tell his story and give more insights into Kate's life. Frank always was a good guy, the sort of honest copper that we expect, and there was no way I was going to tarnish his memory in any way in this story. After all, Kate and Brett have already had quite enough to cope with in their lives.

Several characters get a proper send-off in this final story. Doctor Henderson makes things right with Charlotte and Will after his dubious position in the second trilogy. Jenna is released from prison and will be reunited with

Piper. Rex Emery makes what I think is the right decision to move on from the guest house and use his compensation money to rebuild a new life with his family. Milo, who appears to be nothing but an annoyance at the start of the story, proves himself to be brave, courageous and level-headed. Kate secures her reputation at Morecambe Police once again by working with Charlotte to find out who killed David Brewer and murdered her father. Isla and George get to retire - at last! Isla deserves a medal for all she's done to keep that guest house running. Piper and Agnieszka get to set their lives back on track, and Jon Rogers retires after many years of faithful service in the library archive.

Finally, of course, we have Charlotte who has one final surprise tucked up her sleeve. She arrived in Morecambe recovering from a breakdown and a career implosion. She ends the series having taken back her power. She's carved out a whole new niche for herself and discovered a skill for writing. But, she chooses not to work for the newspaper because Milo has made her think about the future of the media. Instead, she collaborates with Josh to become a true-crime reporter, and take control of her fate. Charlotte finally sees the formidable woman that she is and sets herself up for a very happy and illustrious new career.

I hope you feel that all the loose ends got tied up neatly. I know how frustrating it can be when a series ends, and it just dies out with a whimper. When I write my endings, I'm always mindful of a TV series I watched called *Six Feet Under*. To my tastes, it had the best ending of any TV show to date; it was so perfect the way it concluded the journeys of all the characters in whom viewers had invested so much time. You can watch it on YouTube. It still makes me cry every time I see it, but that's the way to end a long-running TV series.

There are just a couple more things to say about this final trilogy before we close the door on Charlotte Grayson and her pals.

As ever, I rename some locations just to steer clear of any legal bother. Adventure Kingdom is, of course, modelled on the wonderful and much-missed Frontierland pleasure park in the resort. The caravan park I use in this series is modelled on the fabulous Ocean Edge site. I call it Golden Beaches Holiday Park in this series. The same park makes an appearance in the second book of the Don't Tell Meg Trilogy, and you'll discover why I made it a fictional holiday park when you find out what happens to Pete Bailey and friends while he's staying there. My rule of thumb in these books is to create fictional locations where bad stuff happens; I don't want to be causing problems for local businesses after all.

Gog's spectacles were based on the old UK National Health glasses that kids used to have to wear. My older brother and my younger sister both had to wear NHS glasses. If memory serves me correctly, you were given a choice of brown, blue or pink frames. The experience scarred my brother and sister for life, they hated having to wear those glasses. By the time I found out I was short-sighted, I was able to access the slightly cooler John Lennon style frames. Of course, we should never bemoan our lot. We were privileged and lucky to be able to access free spectacles in the first place, but I did let out an inward cheer when my kids needed spectacles and I discovered that you can now get cool frames for your kids via the NHS.

This is the second time I've used a scrapyard as a location in my books, though the drama comes from different sources. My one and only (to date!) US-based story, *Now You See Her,* has a dramatic scene set in a scrapyard. When

I was a kid, my dad ran and fixed up old bangers because we couldn't afford new cars. I spent much time as a child roaming breakers' yards with my dad, scavenging for old parts which would keep our car on the road. They're a place of fascination for me, though I hasten to add, they're a lot safer in real-life than they are in my books.

Let's save the final paragraph for The Winter Gardens and the RNLI - the Royal National Lifeboat Institution - both integral parts of life in Morecambe. The Winter Gardens is a charity that relies on visitors and donations, so please do support them if you're ever in Morecambe and following Charlotte's trail. See if you can find the theatre seat which I sponsored here, too; you'll know it when you see it. I highly recommend the backstage tours if you're able to fit one in.

As for the RNLI, it's not the first time they've had to rescue Charlotte. The RNLI building is a prominent sight as you take a walk along the seafront, and the service they provide along that hazardous stretch of coastline is invaluable and exceptional. So, if you get the chance whilst visiting, do as Charlotte does, and drop a few coins into their collection boxes.

So, that's the Morecambe Bay series completed. I have loved writing these characters, visiting Morecambe to research my locations and interacting with readers who enjoy these stories. Charlotte is now off to enjoy a calm and successful career as an author. I think she deserves it after all she's been through.

Paul Teague

December 2021

ACKNOWLEDGMENTS

In memory of Julie Cordiner, who edited the first six books in this series.

———

My thanks to the following readers, without whom this final trilogy would have been riddled with errors ...

Charlie & Diane Creek
Claire Garner
Terry Rowe
Louise Povey
Mark Swindlehurst
Angela Brennan
Angela Hardy
Daphne Campbell
Allie Byott
Maria Brodowicz
Paula Rollins
David Berg

Alex Mellor
Geoff Miles
Ann Greenwood
Manual Rohinesh
Doug 'Kosh' Williamson
Siobhan McKenna
Peter Devenish
David Delano
Norma Grogan
Michael Murphy
Karen Matsui
Wendy Hewitt
Judy Johnson
Sam Stokes
Dee Gott
Aline Boundy

ALSO BY PAUL J. TEAGUE

No More Secrets

So Many Lies

Two Years After

Friends Who Lie

Now You See Her

ABOUT THE AUTHOR

Hi, I'm Paul Teague, the author of the Don't Tell Meg trilogy as well as several other standalone psychological thrillers such as One Last Chance, Dead of Night and Now You See Her.

I'm a former broadcaster and journalist with the BBC, but I have also worked as a primary school teacher, a disc jockey, a shopkeeper, a waiter and a sales rep.

I've read thrillers all my life, starting with Enid Blyton's Famous Five series as a child, then graduating to James Hadley Chase, Harlan Coben, Linwood Barclay and Mark Edwards.

If you love those authors then you'll like my thrillers too.

Let's get connected!
https://paulteague.net

This is a work of fiction. Names, characters, businesses, places, events and incidents are either the products of the author's imagination or used in a fictitious manner. Any resemblance to actual persons, living or dead, or actual events is purely coincidental.

All rights reserved. No part of this book may be reproduced or transmitted in any form or by any electronic or mechanical means, including photocopying, recording or by any information storage and retrieval system, without the written permission of the Author, except where permitted by law.

Copyright © 2022 Paul Teague writing as Paul J. Teague

All rights reserved

CPSIA information can be obtained
at www.ICGtesting.com
Printed in the USA
BVHW081402301221
625196BV00008B/181